GAI

A Crime in Barbados

By Kayio Beckles

To Danielle, without whose encouragement and support at every step, this would not have been possible

Table of Contents

Prologue..1

Chapter 1 3

Chapter 2 18

Chapter 3 33

Chapter 4 55

Chapter 5 70

Chapter 6 82

Chapter 7 90

Chapter 8 110

Chapter 9 125

Chapter 10 142

Chapter 11 172

Chapter 12 191

Chapter 13 219

Chapter 14 233

Epilogue 260

A Few Words From The Author.................................264

Prologue

Jeremy turned off the car radio because he couldn't concentrate on anything the announcer was saying.

He had turned it on in the first place to listen to the cricket commentary - West Indies were playing Australia in Antigua - hoping it would help him relax. But he knew even then that it would have been futile. The only thing on his mind was his wife. Was she even alive?

He barely thought about the waitress. The news reports stated she was "missing in suspicious circumstances" but he had a few more details than that. The names of he and his wife were even mentioned in the broadcast.

He was sitting in his friend's Mazda Lantis which was parked outside of Esso Black Rock, a service station and convenience store just off Spring Garden Highway, the major traffic artery leaving the capital, Bridgetown, heading North. It was two thirteen in the afternoon, thirteen minutes past the arranged meeting time.

The store was busy with its usual parade of university students, bus conductors and taxi drivers. Jeremy had been counting on the presence of a sizeable crowd when he agreed to meet at this location.

"Why is this happening?" he whispered to himself. Part of him was still clinging to the hope that everything that had happened in the last seventy-two hours was an elaborate prank at his expense. Things like this only happened in movies. It couldn't be real.

But he remembered the blood. The blood was real.

Chapter 1

West Indies vs Sri Lanka
Galle, Sri Lanka

Day 1 Report
*Brian Lara returned to Test cricket with a brilliant hundred
on the opening day of the series, helping West Indies to 316
for 3.*

*His unbeaten 117 has been characterised by confidence and
an overall sense of adventure.*

Tuesday, November 13th, 2001

Even though it was November, Jeremy was surprised by how chilly the night had become.

He guessed that the temperature might be as low as twenty-two degrees Celsius, which was relatively cool for a Barbadian night. The fact that he was naked didn't help.

He walked slowly forward, shoulders hunched, hands slightly out in front, held in the way a man might if he was about to choke someone. Which, in a way, he was.

The lawn he was crossing was well maintained in the way that only the wealthy or the social climbing middle-class can afford. The latter category applied in this case.

Jeremy was very familiar with the layout of the house and land. He knew there wasn't a dog or an alarm system and was also very aware of the narrow corridor of opportunity between the motion detecting security lights fixed at all corners of the one-story house. If he was careful, he could walk in a straight line towards the house without triggering any of the two nearest lights. This was important since it wouldn't do for any neighbours to see a naked man creeping around in the dark. This was Rowans Park, St. George after all, an upper middle class development in the centre of the island. While instances of break-ins had declined in the previous few years, residents were still quite wary of possible intruders. And most definitely of the naked, creeping variety.

Jeremy was confident that he would not be seen as long as he was careful. He remembered a Marvel Comics character Nightcrawler - one of the mutant X-Men - who became almost invisible in shadows due to the indigo colour of his skin. Creeping around in the night, clad only in his naked, chocolate-coloured skin, made Jeremy feel as if he could be that mutant.

Like so many Barbadian houses, this one greeted visitors with a beautiful mahogany front door with a close to impenetrable dead-bolt lock. Except for a nervous spell in the early part of the 1990's when the creatively dubbed *'dead-bolt man'* was making a mockery of the security in the Parks and Terraces, the well-to-do in Barbados were relatively safe behind secure locks and bolts. Backdoors were a different story, however.

Jeremy surveyed the aluminium, louvered backdoor in front of him. The polycarbonate shutters were set in two segments one on top of the other. The lower segment was closed and Jeremy knew that pushing home the operating handle would lock these types of louvers. The upper segment was partially open.

It should have been an easy matter to simply open the upper shutters fully, reach in with his slender arm, unlock the door from inside and *voilà*. But any insomniac will tell you that if a droplet of water falls in the kitchen sink at one o'clock a.m., it might as well be a gunshot. So he had to be very, very quiet.

Moving stealthily, Jeremy opened the shutters so that they sat horizontally. This simple act took more than a minute due to the extreme care he took not to make any sound. Twice during the process he paused when he thought he was being too noisy. He then pushed his right arm through the space and reached down to the lock.

He fumbled for the locking clip for a while, but he fumbled quietly.

Jeremy was aware of every sound in the area.

He could hear the crickets chirping in the grass of the empty lot next door. He had read somewhere that if you count the number of chirps a cricket makes in a specific period of time, you could work out the atmospheric temperature. Jeremy couldn't remember the required formula at that moment, but he didn't need it. He already knew that it was too damned cold for a naked man to be parading outdoors in St. George!

He could hear the sound of a radio in a nearby house and even made out that it was the annoyingly flat, mono sound of an AM station. After a few seconds he recognised the song being played: something about the different ways Barbadians (or Bajans as they refer to themselves) of the various social classes laugh - an early example of Calypso music.

Jeremy had time to hear a verse and a bit of the chorus before he found the locking clip and turned it slowly. It rotated without a sound.

Jeremy took a deep breath before setting about his next task: opening the door. He had never come across a door of any kind that opened completely quietly in his life, with one exception. As a child, he owned a Sony stereo with a double tape deck. Under each deck was a sticker that proudly proclaimed *Silent Action* - which he assumed meant that when you pressed eject, the lid was supposed to open smoothly and quietly. Like all reliable Japanese technology, it did just that, much to the fascination of the then twelve year old Jeremy.

He slowly turned the lock until he was sure that the latch was released from its cylinder. Once more there was no sound. Ironically, this was due to the lock being well lubricated and maintained, so that the occupants could sleep in peace knowing that their middle-class belongings and lives were well protected by correctly working security devices.

He put his one hundred and seventy-five pound frame flat against the door and pushed firmly but smoothly. It held for a moment before swinging in with a slight rubbing noise. He froze for one full minute, listening for any signs from inside the house that he had been heard.

No house is ever completely silent. Even if he hadn't already known, he could tell he was in the kitchen from the quiet hum of the refrigerator to his right. He detected a slight scratching sound above him - most likely insects or some other vermin living in the roof crawl space. There was also a dripping faucet, but nothing to indicate any other unwanted movement in the house.

Jeremy pulled in the door behind him, just enough to prevent it from swinging in the wind. He took two steps into the kitchen and stopped when he realised he was being too noisy. His bare feet were sticking to the kitchen tiles and making a tacky sound at each step. It wasn't very loud, but at four minutes past one in the morning...

He looked over to his left into what was obviously the dining room with a mahogany dinette set and ornate cabinet displaying shelves of never-to-be-used gift items which screamed '*we got married and had lots of generous friends*'.

But Jeremy noticed these only in passing. What really caught his eye was the thick carpet running from the threshold of the kitchen into the dining room. From where he was standing there was about four feet of tile before the beginning of the carpeted area. At five feet ten inches, Jeremy fancied his chances of covering this distance in one giant step.

He swivelled his body to the left towards the dining room and in one motion made a half step, half jump on to the carpet.

As he landed, and tried to keep his balance, he had a sudden flashback of playing hopscotch when he was much younger. When your opponent owned squares two through six, and you were trying to reach seven or eight from square one, the necessary leap was similar to the one he had just made.

He smiled and almost chuckled from the memory, but considering that he had not played the game in more than twenty years, and more especially his current predicament, the sudden humour was misplaced. The chuckle was quickly suppressed.

Jeremy made an exploratory step and noted with some satisfaction that the degree of stealth increased considerably on the carpet.

He walked through the dining room and turned right into a large sitting room, finding himself facing the corridor towards the bedrooms and bathrooms. Then he noticed the strip of plastic covering the carpet throughout the corridor. It was the carpet runner used to ensure that carpeting in high traffic areas was not worn by trampling feet.

He almost made an audible '*oh oh*'. There was no way to be quiet on that material.

Jeremy was not about to be thwarted at this stage in the proceedings. *Think, think, think* he thought to himself.

Then he saw it. The runner did not actually extend all the way to the walls. There was almost six inches of exposed carpet on each side.

He placed his right foot in the uncovered space at right and then did the same with his left foot to the other side, straddling the width of the carpet runner, and started walking.

Slowly walking down the corridor in this way, he had another flashback to a game where the person who was '*it*' instructed you to walk in different ways until one player had crossed the playground and reached '*it*'.

He tried to remember the name of that game for a few seconds but quickly lost interest in the answer when he reached the bedroom at the end of the corridor.

There she was.

Jeremy had seen the movie *The Fabulous Baker Boys* in which every scene with Michelle Pfeiffer seemed to have been shot with a different camera and by a different director from the rest of the movie. She was just so lovely, everything else paled in comparison. The vision of the woman lying in the bed had a similar effect.

There was just enough moonlight pouring through partially opened curtains to frame the scene for him.

Lying on her back, head turned to one side, displaying a long, graceful neck, but only allowing a glimpse of her boyishly cropped hair; one arm lying on her flat stomach, the other thrown casually at her side; a T-shirt covering very little of her toned thighs; one leg bent slightly at the knee, revealing part of a well-developed calf muscle, the other leg extended elegantly; painted, manicured toes pointing like a dancer's.

He had seen her so many times before, and yet the sight never failed to suck an entire breath out of him.

Jeremy crossed the room with three quick steps, leapt on to the bed straddling her, and grabbed her throat with his right hand while covering her mouth with his left. Her eyes flashed open, initially conveying confusion, which quickly transformed into what could have been fear, but could also have been surprise. She started to squirm, but barely budged him.

"Don't scream, and stop struggling," he whispered harshly.

The eyes continued flashing fear or surprise or whatever it was, with no indication that the woman heard or understood what he had said. She continued struggling.

"Do you believe that I could snap your neck like a twig?"

For just one moment, Jeremy thought a look crossed her face which said, *'actually, I don't think you could'*. But like a wisp of cloud passing in front of a full moon, the look was gone before he knew for sure that it had ever been there. She nodded slowly and stopped squirming.

"Good, I'll remove my hand," and Jeremy took his left hand from her mouth. She licked her lips, and, impossibly, became even more stunning in the moonlight.

Jeremy continued in a half-whisper. "Let me bring you up-to-date. I outweigh you by at least thirty pounds, I'm twice as strong as you are and I have some leverage in this position. I could go on, but I imagine you see the point. So forget what you see in the movies, you are not going to overpower me, okay?"

The last word was not completely out of his mouth, before the woman bucked like an unbroken thoroughbred, and sent him crashing face first into the wall beyond.

He ricocheted back onto the bed, still on top of her, no longer holding her throat, but instead covering his nose with both hands. The next sound emitted was muffled but decidedly Bajan.

"Rasshole!" pronounced as if it was two words.

The woman bolted into a sitting position, almost pushing Jeremy off of the bed in the process. She reached for the hands covering his nose, words tumbling from her mouth.

"Oh God, Jeremy, are you all right?" she asked, trying to pull his hands away from his face.

"Dammit," was the muffled response.

"Let me see it," she said, sounding less concerned, and more amused.

"Not funny, Rachel" Jeremy said from under his hands.

"I know it's not," Rachel said, smiling outright now. "Come on, let me see it."

Jeremy allowed his hands to be pulled away from his face with the reluctance of a pupil submitting a test paper that he knew he had failed.

Rachel inspected his lips and nose. Jeremy flinched every time she touched him. "Come on, it's not that bad. You've got a boo-boo on your lip but nothing's broken."

"Easy for you to say, it wasn't your face remodelling the wall."

Rachel smiled, "Oh honey, I'm so sorry. I didn't mean to beat you up like that."

"You didn't beat me up; you just got a lucky shot, again," Jeremy said sulkily.

"I'll let you win next time."

"Don't do me any favours," Jeremy said touching his nose gingerly.

Rachel started running her hand through his chest hair. "But I want you to win, JP. You're supposed to overpower me and take advantage of this poor, helpless maiden."

"Helpless my ass," Jeremy said pointing to his lip for emphasis.

Rachel leaned forward and kissed the bruise on his upper lip. "Oh don't sulk, honey, let me make it better," she said lapsing into baby talk.

"Okay, okay, Rachel, I'm fine, all right," Jeremy said, moving his head around to avoid the healing lips.

"Why are you naked?" Rachel asked suddenly.

"Well, I've noticed over the years that clothes tend to get in the way of sex, and…"

"I mean, where are your clothes?"

"Oh, they're in the car."

"I didn't hear the car," Rachel said, sitting up with a puzzled look. "Where is it?"

"Over in Fourth Avenue."

Rachel looked shocked. "You left your car there? And walked home naked?"

"Yeah, the things I do for you, and our adventurous love life."

Rachel paused for a second, still with that shocked expression on her face before collapsing backwards onto the bed laughing.

"I don't believe you," she said haltingly through her mirth.

"Yeah, well a couple of neighbours might not believe me either."

"Did someone see you?"

"Of course not. I'm Nightcrawler"

"Who?"

"Forget it"

Rachel sat up and caressed Jeremy's face.   There was still a hint of humour left in her eyes, but it shared the space with a few other emotions.   That combination enhanced her beauty.   Even after two years of marriage Jeremy found his wife lovelier every day.

"How weird are we?" Rachel asked.

"Not weird at all," Jeremy replied. "Let's see. Last Tuesday, we made love in a restaurant bathroom in the middle of the day; a couple of weeks ago, *you* broke into the house and raped *me*; and let's not forget the dinner table fingering incident at your grandmother's house. All in all, we're not weird at all."

Rachel smiled. "Hmmm. Maybe weird is the wrong word," she said, pushing Jeremy off of her. "Get up. Let's go get your car."

Jeremy sat up to allow Rachel the space to get up. She pulled her T-shirt over her head, and headed for the door.

"Uh, Mrs. Phillips," Jeremy called.

"Yes, Mr. Phillips," she answered, pausing at the door, glancing back over her shoulder, sensuously.

"Aren't you getting dressed, ma'am?"

Rachel winked. "Where's the fun in that? Let's go."

Chapter 2

West Indies vs Pakistan
Peshawar, Pakistan

Day 1 Report
Pakistan dominated the first day's play, dismissing the West Indies for only 151. West Indies struck back early to leave Pakistan on 14 for 1 at the close.

A key moment in this test is likely to be the eventual introduction of West Indies' debutant leg spinner Rawle Lewis. How Pakistan's spin-adept batsmen respond may determine the tone of this match.

Monday, November 17th, 1997

The Outfield Sports Bar and Restaurant, on the South coast of Barbados, had, in a short time after opening in early 1997, become Jeremy's *'local'*, even though he neither lived nor worked particularly close to the establishment.

Unassuming glass front doors opened into a welcome foyer, from where patrons could view the entire interior expanse of the hexagonal shaped restaurant.

Seating for one hundred and twenty diners was tastefully designed and cleverly laid out on two levels for the most efficient use of the space. Twenty plasma screen televisions invariably showing multiple sporting events adorned the walls. The largest viewing surface was a massive projector screen directly above the bar area.

The wall behind the bar was finished with an end-to-end mirror decorated around the edges with etched images of various sportsmen. Sharing the walls with the televisions were framed posters depicting superstars of sports ranging from cricket, soccer and rugby to baseball, NFL football and ice hockey. Any leftover wall space was filled with glass cases housing autographed team jerseys.

The dining and drinks menus were littered with items named after sporting elements and puns. Jeremy's favourite was the *Hit & Rum*, which was bread-pudding with a hot spiced rum sauce.

In summary, The Outfield was a cathedral for televised sports enthusiasts.

On that Monday evening in November, Jeremy was worshipping at the bar of said cathedral with his main prayer buddy Curt James, who was known to all as Tiberius.

He had done nothing to earn that moniker other than befriend a Star Trek fan called Jeremy Phillips when they were both seven years old.

Jeremy had made the connection between his new friend's name and that of the first captain of the science fiction series – James T. Kirk. That 'T' stood for Tiberius.

Tiberius was a good-looking, fair skinned black man of average height, usually sporting a shaved head and John Lennon glasses. He had been chubby as a child but by 1997 at twenty-eight years old, he had converted most of the excess weight to muscle. He was a laid back, social animal with the most infectious laugh possible. He was always up for a drink and was often the life of the party without even trying.

The restaurant was surprisingly busy for a Monday evening. Fifty or so patrons were sprinkled throughout the dining area. Another seven, all men, sat at the bar, including Jeremy and Tiberius, each of whom was on his second Heineken.

Both of them had come straight from work so were still dressed formally. Tiberius was wearing a short-sleeved white shirt with the word *TravelWise* embroidered in green on the breast pocket. He had removed his tie, leaving the top two buttons of the shirt open. Jeremy was still wearing a stylish blue and grey tie which complemented a light blue long-sleeved shirt.

The Portland Trailblazers were toying with the Dallas Mavericks in an early season NBA game on the big screen in front of them, but the guys were discussing cricket.

"That team is an embarrassment to their legacy, to West Indians everywhere and to themselves!" Tiberius spat, punctuating the last word by slamming his empty beer bottle onto the counter.

"I'm not following. How do you really feel about the West Indies team?" Jeremy asked.

"Screw you, JP. That's how I feel."

"After just two drinks? Sir, I am not that kind of lady!" Jeremy returned.

Tiberius made a rude, sucking noise with his mouth, while making a '*V*' signal with his middle and index fingers towards the bartender, who promptly fished into the chiller for two more cold Heinekens. Tiberius then turned the same hand towards Jeremy, lowering only his index finger.

"Screw. You. Jeremy. Phillips," he reiterated.

Jeremy laughed. "Listen, the boys played nuff shite last night, but if you think I'll let that prevent me from enjoying a beer, you're dead wrong?"

The bartender, who was following most of the conversation from a few feet away, came closer to weigh in. "Look it's only the first day. They got four more to get back in the game."

The bartender was a tall, strapping Trinidadian of East Indian descent who was known as Doc to everyone. He was always eager to discuss cricket, but his views on the state of the sport in the Caribbean were somewhat more optimistic than Tiberius', who was now looking at him incredulously.

"Doc, the West Indies were embarrassed last night. That spinner Mushtaq made it look like they sent a bunch of school boys to Pakistan to play against professionals." This tirade was followed by another rude noise, what Barbadians call 'sucking one's teeth'.

Doc leaned forward on the counter towards Tiberius. "Boy look, Lara, Hooper and Chanderpaul could play spin bowling good enough. They just got to get used to Pakistan conditions. Wait and see by the second innings they gone be beating ball."

Tiberius stared at Doc for a beat then turned to Jeremy and rolled his eyes.

Doc continued, "Hear this, boy. If the West Indies lose this series, every time you come here and I on duty, yuh first drink gone be on me."

"Deal!" Tiberius exclaimed hastily with a big grin, while swivelling his bar-stool in Jeremy's direction.

"Free drinks in our future JP. Well, in my future anyway. I hope Doc ain't planning on leaving The Outfield anytime... look at that red skin thing."

In Barbados, there are many colloquialisms used to describe a person who is the product of an interracial union. Many of them are humorously rude and others are rudely humorous. '*Red*' or '*red skin*' is at the mild end of both scales.

Tiberius was looking past Jeremy towards the entrance of the restaurant. Jeremy turned to follow his gaze and got his first glimpse of his future wife.

She was standing in the doorway looking back over her shoulder, speaking to someone Jeremy couldn't see, giving him a few moments to absorb the scene.

Tall, slim and graceful, posing with that confident air of a woman who knows the effect she has on everyone around her and likes it. Light brown hair, cropped short, caressed smooth, caramel coloured skin. A white strappy blouse rode easily on a simple blue skirt which just brushed the top of her knees exposing long, toned legs. And heels.

Jeremy was already imagining what those heels would feel like against his shoulders when Tiberius popped his fantasy bubble.

"Looks like she got that ass from the darker branches of the family tree."

Jeremy shook his head in mock exasperation but he had in fact noticed the sexy curves of her middle third with some degree of satisfaction.

He was still admiring that segment when she suddenly looked forward and started approaching the bar, catching Jeremy off guard. Their eyes met briefly before Jeremy could look away, betraying the fact that he had been staring. She acknowledged that fact with fleeting hint of a smile.

She reached the bar and sat four stools away from Jeremy's left, leaving her partially obscured from him by two American men who were engrossed in the NBA game.

Jeremy turned and looked straight ahead to catch her reflection in the bar mirror, hoping to make eye contact again. She seemed oblivious to his presence as she chatted with Doc, who now seemed equally oblivious to everyone else at the bar.

"I guarantee that bar service for us is going to suck now," Tiberius quipped. "There's nothing Doc likes more than a sexy young thing. Except maybe a sexy young thing cooking curried goat."

Jeremy sighed and said, "I'm ignoring your pseudo-racist pseudo-joke because I think that girl is checking me out."

They both looked at the mirror and watched Doc exhibiting remarkable flourish in drink mixing while chatting with the woman, who seemed genuinely engrossed in the conversation.

Tiberius chuckled. "I have never seen so much style and flare go into mixing a drink, look at him," he said as Doc tossed an ice cube over his shoulder into an empty glass behind him. The woman at the bar seemed mildly impressed.

Tiberius swivelled his stool towards Jeremy. "Right, now back to you. Which girl exactly do you think is checking you out? Certainly not the one at this bar making goo-goo eyes at Tom Cruise. You know, in *Cocktail*. Played a bartender..."

Jeremy cut him off. "Ti, I understood the Tom Cruise reference, now shut up. I'm telling you, it's really subtle but she's checking me out."

They again looked at the mirror. Doc had pulled himself away from her to fill drink orders for the wait staff. The woman was now busily opening a small black purse and removing an even smaller black phone which was ringing.

"Jeremy, if she's checking you out, I have never seen it done more subtly. In fact that may be the subtlest thing I have ever seen," Tiberius said with mock solemnity.

"Ti, trust me on this."

Tiberius stroked his chin which was just beginning to show signs of day-old stubble. "Well, I've been wrong about this sort of thing before where you're concerned. But by the way, how do you know she's not Doc's girl?"

Jeremy chewed on that possibility for a moment, recognising that he had periodically heard Doc refer to a girlfriend but had never met her. "Hmmm, I didn't think about that."

"I'll find out for you my friend. Doc!" Tiberius yelled before Jeremy could stop him. The bartender had been walking towards the woman but now reluctantly diverted to the guys.

"Ready for another round already? You two are going kind of fast for a Monday night," he said leaning on the counter smiling.

"Thanks for the update, mom," Tiberius snapped. "Who is that girl at the bar?"

"Oh you mean Rachel? She's a new customer; started coming 'round recently. She's a friend of the new waitress, Susan. Her." He ended with a nod of his head towards a short, plump waitress who was now approaching the bar carrying a tray with three empty glasses. She exchanged a few words and a smile with Rachel before continuing to the wait station at the end of the bar.

Doc returned his attention to the guys. "And when I say friend, I mean, *friend*." The second '*friend*' was emphasised with a slow nod of his head and a squint of his eyes.

"Doc, are you saying she's playing for the *other* team?" Tiberius asked, not even trying to conceal his amusement.

"I don't have any proof or nothing, but that's what people saying," Doc revealed with a smile and walked away towards the wait station.

"You know Jeremy, you could be right. Maybe she was checking you out after all. Maybe she saw your slender body and thought you were a chick," Tiberius said before erupting into his signature laugh, causing everyone in the immediate area to look his way and smile.

Rachel, who was still on the phone, looked to her right towards Tiberius and then turned her gaze forward to the mirror where her eyes locked with Jeremy's once more. This time the smile was unmistakable. Jeremy smiled back, and made a decision.

"Tiberius my friend, sometimes a man's gotta do what a man's gotta do," Jeremy announced as he motioned to get Doc's attention. The bartender made the '*one moment*' signal with his index finger while he prepared a round for three guys at the far corner of the bar.

"And what exactly does a man gotta do, JP?"

"Build bridges, climb mountains, that sort of thing. I'm going to climb me a mountain."

Doc appeared in front of them. "Yes, gentlemen."

Jeremy leaned towards the bartender. "I'd like to buy a drink for the young lady when she's ready for her next one."

Doc grinned. "Man, you really like a challenge."

"He's a mountain climber," Tiberius volunteered.

Doc gave Tiberius a knowing look and walked over to Rachel.

Jeremy followed the exchange in the mirror. She was no longer on the phone and was about half way through her drink. Doc said a few words to her before indicating Jeremy and Tiberius with a motion of his left thumb. She made no attempt to follow his direction, but instead focussed on the mirror where she found Jeremy's eyes. Again. And she smiled. Again.

This time Tiberius noticed. "What the hell am I seeing?" he hissed under his breath. "How did you do that? You've been practicing obeah or something?" he queried, referring to a type of Caribbean sorcery.

Jeremy turned towards Tiberius. "Hey, maybe I'm just lucky. Or maybe my equipment is better than yours; my mountain climbing equipment that is."

Tiberius was now looking over Jeremy's shoulder. "Well, get ready Mohammed, 'cause the mountain is coming to you."

Jeremy swivelled around in his barstool to find Rachel standing next to him.   He started to stand, but she stopped him by touching his shoulder.

"Don't get up," she said with exactly the type of sultry, smoky voice he imagined she would have.   "I just wanted to thank you for the drink offer but one is my limit on a work night. I'm Rachel by the way," she held out her hand.

Jeremy accepted it.   "It's great to meet you, Rachel. I'm Jeremy and this is Tiberius."

Tiberius also shook her hand. "Hello Rachel. *You* can call me Curt."

Rachel smiled and looked puzzled at the same time. "Hi Curt.   So what's with '*Tiberius*'?"

"Why don't you sit with us and let me tell you the story of the asshole who gave me that name.   Here's a spoiler: he's at this bar" Tiberius said, and began to stand to offer her his stool.

Rachel giggled.   "That does sound like quite a story, but I really have to go. I'm really sorry to miss it, though."

Jeremy allowed his disappointment to show. "I'm sorry too. Hopefully we'll run into each other again."

There was the faintest of smiles as she opened her purse to drop the phone inside.

"You really shouldn't leave it to chance," she said and produced a business card from the purse. "Call me when next you get the urge to buy a stranger a drink."

With that, she turned and headed for the exit, pausing only to wave goodbye to Susan the waitress. Jeremy and Tiberius followed the path of her departure before simultaneously looking down at the business card.

There was the logo for Warrens Motors, an auto dealer followed by:

Rachel Bailey
Senior Sales Executive – Land Rover

Tiberius was the first to speak. "I don't know how you do it. It's not like you're any major looker and you've got no muscle tone to speak of. Plus, I swear you have got the worst game I have ever seen. And yet there's always some fine specimen throwing herself at you. Tell me the truth: do you have a massive bird?"

Jeremy laughed as he signalled to the bartender. "Tiberius, my friend shall we have one last round?"

"Yeah, yeah, sure. Seriously man, it's got to be about your dick. Maybe women have a newsletter with a column dedicated to it. The headline would read: '*He's tiny like a hummingbird, but he's got an ostrich in his pants*'. Wait. Hummingbird? Is that your secret? Does your bird hum? Come on, whip it out and let's have a listen. Let's all listen!"

Chapter 3

West Indies vs Sri Lanka
Galle, Sri Lanka

Day 2 Report
A dramatic West Indies batting collapse pulled Sri Lanka
back into the match. After starting the day on 316 for 3,
West Indies were bowled out after lunch for 448.

In reply, Sri Lanka were 103 for 1 when bad light stopped
play. The home team ended the day in a much better
position that they could have hoped at the start.

Wednesday, November 14th, 2001

Jeremy was parked outside of his office listening to the sports news just after eight o'clock in the morning.

He was catching up with the previous night's cricket scores, which he had missed because:

1. There was no live international television coverage for this series;
2. He had worked until half past midnight finalising a presentation for a potential new client;
3. Instead of heading straight home and to bed, he parked three avenues away from his house and played naked burglar;

4. His wife insisted on playing naked car thieves to retrieve his car, and

5. Role playing would be pointless without the end game, which needed two rounds and forty-seven minutes to complete.

The last four reasons also explained why he was so exhausted that morning.

He was operating on three hours sleep, and his presentation was at eleven that morning. Every muscle was actively complaining about the lack of proper recovery time after last night's exertions.

Jeremy looked into his rear view mirror to inspect his lip. There was definitely some swelling there despite Rachel's assurances to the contrary. He touched it and flinched slightly. Not an ideal look for a new client pitch.

He got out of his car, did a full body stretch and started towards the front door of Archer Chandler Advertising, where he had worked for seven years. His recent promotion to Creative Services Manager meant that not only did he have final say on all advertising artwork and copy, but he also had a key role in wooing new clients. His background as a graphic designer who blossomed into an account executive and then more recently an account relations manager was ideal experience for his current responsibilities.

ACA was located just outside of Bridgetown in Belleville, an area with a unique history. It was created on sixty acres of land as a residential neighbourhood in the 1880's, and was considered to be one of the first examples in Barbados of proper town planning. The first residents consisted exclusively of white middle and upper class families that were relocating from the heart of the capital.

Over the years, due in no small part to its proximity to Bridgetown, Belleville gradually evolved into a lively commercial centre consisting of a number of businesses in the medical, insurance, advertising and other arenas. A handful of residential homes still remained interspersed among the commercial entities, making for an interesting dynamic at times.

The agency was housed in a restored colonial-styled two story building. Across the street was a tiny structure which could probably fit into two rooms of his unassuming St. George home. It was made of wood and limestone and was of the indigenous chattel design. Well maintained, it sat as proudly as it had for almost one hundred years, predating every business in the area by at least half a century. It was probably the smallest of the remaining residential homes in the area.

In seven years, Jeremy had only ever known two persons to live there: an older woman who spent most mornings reading a newspaper in the window, and her teenage son, whose one absolutely consistent characteristic was a red scarf he unfailingly wore on his head like a bonnet.

Jeremy had once made what he thought was a connection with his work neighbours. In the second half of 1995, not too long after he started at ACA, the Caribbean was experiencing a surprisingly active hurricane season. Even though Barbados itself was not directly struck by any of the nineteen storms that formed that year, bouts of high winds and flooding were regular occurrences.

During a particularly windy September morning, Jeremy sat in his office and saw the wooden shingles which comprised the roof of his neighbour's house flapping wildly in the wind and start to pull away from their straps.

Jeremy rushed across the street in time to find the old lady and her son outside, trying to determine the cause of all the noise coming from their roof. Eventually a small team of ACA employees, led by Jeremy, worked to secure the wayward shingles just before the clouds burst and unleashed torrential rain for the next sixteen hours.

A few days later, Jeremy convinced Martin Chandler – the 'C' in ACA - to allocate $5,000 to have his neighbour's roof completely restored. For a while after that, the old lady was his biggest fan, waving animatedly and calling to him from her window daily. Her son would just nod to Jeremy on their rare encounters.

Eventually status quo reigned. The old lady returned to her daily window newspaper readings, barely acknowledging her neighbours. Her son's nod became less perceptible. Sadly, Jeremy could no longer even recall their names.

On the Wednesday morning of his presentation as Jeremy reached the front door of the ACA building, the young man across the street was leaving home, jumping on a child's bicycle and peddling away in his red bonnet. He nodded mildly at Jeremy, who nodded back at his work neighbour.

Jeremy entered the building and headed to his office, exchanging morning pleasantries with the reception and administrative staff along the way. No one asked about his swollen lip.

As expected, the creative team was largely absent since many had left the office after midnight working on material for the day's presentation. He figured they would start to filter in by nine o'clock or so, but until then the back offices would be eerily quiet, which was precisely what he needed.

He entered his office, closing the door behind him and dropped into his plush leather recliner. He had just leaned back with his eyes closed when his desk phone rang. He sighed and leaned forward to check the caller ID, noting that it was his direct line. The display showed *'unknown number'* tempting Jeremy to ignore the call, but instead he exhaled heavily and answered.

"Jeremy Phillips, can I help you?"

"You made it in," answered his wife's smoky tone. "How are you feeling, sweetie?"

"Like I've been wrestling with a wild beast from the pits of hell itself."

"That's not a nice thing to say about me. I'm actually from the pastures of St. John."

Jeremy smiled. "Are you on your cell phone, honey?"

"Yeah. I'm standing outside of my building to get some privacy. I wanted to wish you good luck with your appointment today."

"Thanks babe, but you wished me luck when you left home this morning, so I'm sure there's more. Let's hear it?"

Rachel giggled. "You know me too well. Do you remember Susan Farrell?"

Jeremy thought about the name. "Susan Farrell. That name rings a bell, like someone I've met…"

"Of course you've met her. We were really tight back in the day. Was kind of on the heavy side. Worked briefly as a waitress at The Outfield…"

"Oh right. You mean Fat-Suey."

Rachel made a disapproving clicking noise with her tongue. "You know, I could kill Tiberius for that Fat-Suey nonsense. Anyway, she's not really plump anymore. Looks quite hot actually."

"Oh really? When did you see her?"

"She was our first customer this morning. Well, not her actually. She was with a guy called Barrington Shorey. Do you know that name?"

"Maybe. Sounds familiar."

"Anyway, he was looking to buy a new Range Rover Sport."

Jeremy whistled. "Isn't that like half a million dollars?"

"Just about."

"Is he buying it for her?"

"I don't think so, but she seemed to have some influence over the decision. That's why they came here to me rather than to the Mercedes or BMW dealers."

"So Fat-Suey's caught a big fish, so to speak."

"Quit that! Anyway, she introduced him as a friend, so I don't know if they're dating or anything."

"Well, I seem to remember she was your *friend* too, so who knows what *that* means," Jeremy said with fake indignation.

"Don't be jealous," she said playfully. "In fact, that's the whole point of this conversation. You didn't think I called just to gossip, did you."

"Gossip? You? Never!"

"Shut up or I'll cancel this threesome I'm thinking about planning."

For the rest of his life, Jeremy would remember every detail of that exact moment.

The morning was overcast and a little cool by Barbadian standards, so he had not yet powered up the air conditioner unit in the office. He now got up, stepped around his desk, keeping the receiver to his ear, and stretched to reach the remote which was sitting in a cradle on the wall opposite his desk.

He noticed for the first time that the painting on that wall, depicting the extinct Barbados railroad, was a little crooked. He also noticed that there was a housefly lazily crawling on the wall next to the painting.

He switched on the unit and as he returned to his chair, he saw through his window his neighbour sitting in her usual position, leafing through a newspaper while talking on the phone and watching a local talk show on television at the same time.

Sitting again, he noted on his desk there were three yellow file folders each bearing the Olympio Lottery logo followed by the words 'Option A', 'Option B' and 'Option C' respectively. They were neatly positioned side by side, equidistant from each other, exactly as he left them after the previous night's session.

He would always remember that on that morning he was sporting a light grey shirt and black slacks with the same blue and grey tie he was wearing the night he first met Rachel. After that night it had become his lucky tie and he wore it whenever he thought he needed a little intangible help.

His wife's voice was in his ear.

"Hellooooo. Are you still there? Don't you have anything to say?"

"Thank you, lucky tie," was all he could offer.

"What?"

"Nothing, honey."

Jeremy leaned back in his chair hoping the relaxed nature of his posture would extend to his voice.

"So you were saying something about, what was it? A threesome or something?"

Rachel laughed. "Idiot. Anyway, I had a chance to speak to Susan privately and you know what? There's still some type of chemistry going on between us that I'm sure I wasn't imagining. Which started me thinking about that one thing you and I haven't done."

Jeremy was trying his best not to appear too eager. "Okay. So did you mention this to her?"

"Of course not. I had to speak to you first. Plus we didn't have much time to chat like that. But if you're okay with the general idea, I could meet up with her for a drink or something and get a sense of what's possible."

Jeremy continued to play it cool. "Good idea, baby. No point in getting your hopes up if there isn't a chance of anything happening."

Rachel burst out laughing. "Jeremy Phillips! Don't you think I know you're chomping at the bit for this to happen? And there you are playing Mr. Smooth. *No point in getting your hopes up,*" she added, imitating his voice.

Jeremy was forced to laugh as well. "Fine, fine, fine. You got me. I'll leave this in your capable hands."

"Have no fear, honey. My hands are legendary in some circles," she said, giggling.

Jeremy sighed heavily, but his face was almost split in two by his grin.

Rachel continued, "Listen, we can talk about this later. I know you have a big day and I also know you'll be amazing. And if all else fails, show them your ass. That always works for me. Love you, sweetie." She blew an audible kiss into the phone.

"Love you too, baby." He hung up.

Jeremy continued to lean back in his recliner, still grinning. He raised his left arm to check on the time: eight twenty-two. His gaze lingered on the watch: a silver Movado SE - a first anniversary gift from his wife.

"I love my wife," Jeremy said aloud to no one.

Casino gambling was illegal in Barbados. Its supposed contribution to criminal elements and society's moral decay were often cited as the main reasons successive governments had enforced this ban.

Local opinion was divided on the merits of this embargo along the lines you would expect. The more conservative and The Church were vocal in their opposition to the very thought of casinos. The more liberal and those with special interests were equally outspoken in the other direction.

However, that didn't mean there was no legal gambling to be enjoyed.

For instance, there had always been organised games of chance for the benefit of charitable and sporting organisations. For many years the Barbados Cricket Association's *Instant Money Game* was the benchmark for success in this type of gambling, its popularity rivalled only by the annual raffles run by the major charities and service organisations.

Scattered across the South and West coasts of the island were a number of establishments featuring slot machines, fittingly referred to as *one armed bandits*. Somehow these spots were all open twenty-four hours a day and most were associated with bars which provided the occasional free beverage for the players. Nothing at all like a casino.

Seedy racing pools, complete with international closed circuit video feeds pervaded specific areas of Bridgetown, allowing dedicated regulars the facility to wager on horse racing from around the world. All above board.

The thriving betting centre for local horse-racing was at the Garrison Savannah racetrack, run by the Barbados Turf Club, the organisation that also produced the first national lottery, Lotto.

Lotto had been an immediate success, channelling unprecedented funds into the club (along with the charities it supported) while creating a few new millionaires among the gambling public.

The Barbados Olympic Association then jumped on that horse-drawn band wagon to create a second national lottery, Olympio, in support of Olympic sports and athletes.

As the new lottery on the block, Olympio's initial rate of adoption by the public was a little slower than anticipated. This resulted in the BOA's thirst for marketing innovation.

The organisation had approached a few of the larger, more established advertising agencies to arrange pitch meetings for the opportunity to handle the lottery's substantial account. Based on the Lotto experience, agencies knew that a lottery account meant considerable concept fees and production charges, along with colossal media buys. It was highly sought after business.

ACA got its opportunity to pitch only after a random Sunday evening meeting over drinks between Jeremy's boss, Martin Chandler, and a board member of the BOA. The catch was they had less than seventy-two hours to put the proposal together.

Jeremy and his team had made the most of that time, fleshing out three solid concept proposals for promoting the lottery, as well as producing the corresponding advertising campaign samples for print, radio and point of sale. They had also conceived of television aspects for the campaigns, but time and budgetary limitations restricted that portion of the presentation to just detailed storyboards.

Jeremy accompanied Martin Chandler to the pitch meeting. As a team, they were a study in contrasts. Martin was a sixty-two year old giant of a man: six feet three inches tall and approaching three hundred pounds. His previously blonde hair was both greying and thinning but he made no attempt to hide either feature.

He was a smooth, charismatic talker - qualities that had served him reasonably well in his previous job as an insurance salesman. He had laboured in that arena enthusiastically but with only moderate success for nineteen long years. But he saved his money and made major sacrifices until finally, at fifty-one years old, he inherited seven million dollars from his departed father and formed ACA with his childhood friend, Peter Archer. Sometimes hard work pays off.

They arrived at the BOA offices about ten minutes early.

Just as they sat down in the waiting area, Jeremy's phone beeped once, indicating a text message. He looked at the display to find a note from Rachel: '*confirmed drinks with susan at cloverleaf after work xxx*'.

The next hour was a blur of handshakes and flip-charts for Jeremy.

There was only a brief wait before they were being directed to a meeting room where three senior managers and two board members were seated around a large oak table.

As usual, Martin did most of the talking, including a masterful opening salvo where he managed to effectively incorporate family details of each BOA official present. Jeremy offered only occasional supporting annotations until the details of the campaign concepts were needed, at which point he took the lead using the necessary audio visual aids.

Afterwards, Jeremy could remember very little of the hour-long discourse. He did recall at one point making reference to '*a threesome of alternative concepts*', which was met with a nervous chuckle from Martin.

That may have been the only time he actually spoke the word '*threesome*' aloud during his presentation, but he certainly thought it every single time he paused in his speech, other than the one time he thought '*ménage à trois*' instead.

As they made the trek back to their cars, Martin was upbeat and optimistic about their performance, speaking highly of Jeremy's contribution and disclosing his opinion that they had just '*swept Olympio off her feet*'. Jeremy barely heard him.

The rest of the work day continued in a similarly distracted vein for

Jeremy.

He was operating on autopilot, resulting in a highly unproductive afternoon session by his standards. He did take the time to meet with his creative team, thanking them for their hard work under a tough deadline and reassuring them that their output was well received by the potential client.

He left the office for home just after five o'clock, checking in en route with Rachel who was still in office. They chatted for a while about his meeting, with Jeremy assuring his wife that at no point did he have to show his ass to anyone. The conversation then inevitably turned to her own upcoming meeting.

"JP, I am actually looking forward to it."

"I'll bet you are."

"Not that, stupid. I mean catching up with Susan this evening. We were really good friends but the way we drifted apart was silly and unnecessary."

"I don't remember that split being as gradual as a '*drift*'..."

"Yeah, but you know what I mean."

"I suppose I do." Jeremy glanced at the digital clock in his car. "What time are your drinks?"

There was a pause on the line, followed by a sharp squeal and the sound of papers rustling. "Oh my God, it's after five. I have like fifteen minutes. I gotta get going."

"Okay baby, I'll let you go. Have a great girls' night out. Go reminisce, exchange recipes and pillow fight or whatever girls do. But don't forget, you're on a mission."

Rachel chuckled. "How could I forget? Listen, I'll probably have dinner there at Cloverleaf. Do you want me to bring you something?"

"Nah, I'll grab something on the way home."

"Okay, I'll see you later then. Honey I know you've had a long, rough day, but you'd better be up when I get home, if you know what I mean. Love you. Ciao."

"Love you too," Jeremy replied and ended the call. He drove for another thirty seconds before making a course correction towards The Outfield. He called to invite Tiberius and discovered he was already on his way there.

Jeremy arrived first and was a few minutes into his first Heineken when Tiberius walked in. He settled next to Jeremy at the bar, noted with satisfaction that Doc was on duty and ordered a Johnny Walker Black and ginger ale.

He turned to Jeremy, paused for a moment before asking, "What the hell is that on your lip?"

———————————————————

Later that night at home, Jeremy idly flipped through television channels looking for something to watch that did not revolve around the 9/11 attacks on America and its aftermath.

Two months had passed since the unprecedented assault on the USA's sense of invulnerability and the news cycles still reverberated with its aftershocks. Tonight all the top stories involved the action in Afghanistan as the rout of the Taliban by US lead coalitions continued.

Jeremy had had enough of the sombre news and eventually settled on an episode of the game show *Jeopardy*, which was one of the programs he watched ritualistically with his wife.

He thought of Rachel and wondered how things were going with her *'meeting'*. It was not the first time that question crossed his mind in the thirty minutes he had been at home. His earlier conversation with Tiberius did not help.

"JP. Buddy. You know I'm as big a fan of deviant lifestyles as the next guy. I'm the president of the deviant lifestyles fan club. I consider the quest for threesomes, foursomes and more-somes to be a God-given right of every healthy-minded male... well maybe God-given isn't strictly appropriate, but you get my drift.

Anyway, even I, the club president, would not risk including my significant other in matters of wanton debauchery. That, my friend, should always remain the purview of drunken spontaneous escapades and opportunistic booty calls.

You can't have your wife planning that shit. What are you thinking? It's not like you're so good-looking or great in the sack that you can afford to let a woman like Rachel, who IS hot and clearly out of your league, experience sex with someone else. Why would you remind her of what actual good sex is like? Plus, she has a history with the girl. That's just asking for trouble.

And as for Fat-Suey – I'm telling you something is wrong with her. I don't think she's right in the head.

By the way, did I use 'purview' correctly earlier?"

Jeremy was quite used to his friend's barstool monologues which were usually performed primarily for his own entertainment. However, this particular faux-rant raised a few doubts in Jeremy's mind. Should he be concerned that Rachel and Susan had a history?

He pushed this thought to one corner of his brain and used the rest of that organ to concentrate on the game show. It was a college championship edition but Jeremy was still being outclassed by the three competing kids and Alex Trebek, who knew everything about everything it seemed.

Jeopardy ended and Jeremy started to get into an episode of *Star Trek: Enterprise* when he heard Rachel's car pull up. Moments later, she walked in carrying a small Styrofoam container in one hand and her handbag in the other. She was wearing the skirt suit she donned half a day before, but as always she looked like she just stepped out of the glamour pages.

"Hello honey," she breathed as she tossed her bag onto a side table and dropped into the sofa next to Jeremy. She leaned into him to plant a soft kiss on his lips. The mild scent of whiskey on her breath mixed intriguingly with the fading bouquet of her body spray, creating what was always for Jeremy an intoxicating elixir.

"I know you got dinner but I brought you some dessert," she said dropping the container onto his lap. "Plus I also brought you this cheesecake," she added seductively.

Jeremy smiled and returned the kiss, savouring her fragrances and textures. They pulled apart after a few moments and sat comfortably looking at each other.

"Well, don't leave me in suspense. How did it go?" Jeremy asked.

"Let me put it this way. Don't make any plans for tomorrow night. You've got an appointment here with two young ladies."

Jeremy stroked his chin and looked upwards thoughtfully. "Two young ladies, huh. Well, that's great and all, but don't you want to join us?"

Rachel gave him a playful slap followed by a deep kiss on his lips.

There were several other slap and kiss combinations before the night was through.

Chapter 4

West Indies vs Pakistan
Peshawar, Pakistan

Day 2 Report 2
*Pakistan squandered the opportunity to build a sizeable
lead over the West Indies, finishing the second day at 246
for 5.*

*West Indies' bowling has been erratic at best, but by taking
five Pakistan wickets, momentum may be with the tourists.*

Tuesday, November 18th, 1997

Jeremy sat in his windowless cubical staring at the business card in his hand, contemplating momentum versus coolness.

He was primarily contemplating Rachel Bailey.

It was nine fifteen in the morning, little more than twelve hours after she introduced herself to him at the Outfield, and he wanted to call her.

He felt he had ended that initial encounter on a high, with Rachel showing what seemed like interest in him. The momentum was with him, so he should go with it and call her, right?

But was it too soon? Would he seem desperate? Shouldn't he play it cool and wait a few days?

Jeremy looked at the business card again, sighed, picked up his phone and dialled. Tiberius answered on the second ring.

"Don't do it, JP."

"Good morning to you too, Ti."

"Whatever. Don't do it I tell you."

"I don't even know what you're talking about."

Tiberius sucked his teeth. "I know you too well Jeremy Phillips. You're trying to decide whether to call the lovely Rachel Bailey right now, rather than wait a few days like I explicitly told you to last night."

"Couldn't I be calling to ensure you made it in to your office on time? After all, you did have more than a few drinks last night."

"Bullshit! You just want to lean on my scholarly knowledge of the fairer sex. So my advice is: don't pursue that girl at all. She is way out of your league, man. In fact, she's so far out, she's approaching my league. I should call her."

"Now why would I want female advice from a divorcee who has never had a relationship that lasted more than one year?"

"Not true, JP. My relationship with my ex-wife lasted fifteen months. If you include the three-month wooing period, and the six-month engagement."

"I think I'm going to call her this morning."

"My ex-wife?"

"I might call her too, now that I have this momentum."

Tiberius' tone became a little more serious.

"Listen, all jokes aside. That girl is a stunner. Call her if you want, whenever you want. But be careful man."

"Why? What are you thinking?"

"Nothing specifically. But in my experience, any woman that hot and available is swarming with issues and baggage. Isn't it enough that she's apparently checking that waitress? What's up with that?"

"Good question."

"Anyway, JP, I'm just saying don't go and get yourself so deep in the honey pot that you can't see when the wasps are coming. But that's just my purview."

"I'll keep all of that in mind, even that bogus honey and wasp thing. But I don't think you're using '*purview*' correctly."

"Sure I am. I'm a perv and that's my view."

"Goodbye Tiberius." Jeremy hung up, cutting off the peals of laughter emanating from the receiver.

He looked at the business card again, twirling it around in his fingers, before whispering to himself, "It's not desperation, it's momentum."

Jeremy dialled quickly so he wouldn't change his mind. A male voice answered after four rings.

"Good morning, Land Rover Sales, this is Matthew Johnson, how can I help you?"

"May I speak to Rachel Bailey, please?"

"She's with a client right now. Do you want to hold or would you like to leave a message."

Jeremy hesitated before saying he'd hold.

He waited for just over a minute, regretting every second of the cheesy hold music that he didn't just leave a message. Then the music was suddenly replaced by a slightly out of breath female voice.

"Sorry to keep you waiting, this is Rachel Bailey, how can I help you?"

"Hello Rachel, this is Jeremy. Phillips. From last night at the Outfield."

"Why hello, Jeremy-Phillips-from-last-night-at-the-Outfield. How are you this morning?"

"I'm great. What about you?"

"I'm fantastic. When I was told someone wanted to wait on the line for me, I assumed it was someone that really wanted information on the new Land Rover Discovery. Instead it's someone that really wants to discover... me." She giggled.

"Well, you could also tell me about the Discovery," was all he could manage.

"Absolutely. But I do have a client outside. How about tomorrow night at the Cloverleaf Lounge? Say seven?"

Jeremy barely paused before replying, "Seven tomorrow works for me."

"Great. It'll be an evening of discovery." She giggled again. "Good bye Jeremy-Phillips-from-last-night-at-the-Outfield. I'll see you tomorrow." And she was gone.

Jeremy leaned back in his chair and loudly exhaled through pursed lips.

He felt a little mentally exhausted from trying to tread water against the tide of that thirty-second conversation. He also felt exhilarated.

"Just go with the flow, Jeremy," he whispered.

After work that evening Jeremy joined Tiberius at the Outfield for dinner. He arrived to find his friend surprisingly sitting at a booth rather than at the bar.

"Okay, who are you hiding from," Jeremy asked as he slid into the booth opposite his friend.

"No one at all. In fact I'm doing the opposite. Now shut up. Here comes our waitress."

Jeremy looked around and saw Rachel's friend Susan approaching. She was dressed in the standard red Outfield polo shirt with tight black jeans which were quite flattering on her plump physique. Her hair was pulled up into a bun and held together by two large wooden pins.

Jeremy returned his gaze to Tiberius mouthing *'What are you doing?'* Tiberius just grinned.

"Good evening gentlemen, welcome to the Outfield. I'm your waitress, Susan. Would you like to see a menu or are you just having drinks?"

Tiberius responded with fake formality, "Why yes Susan, we will be dining tonight."

The waitress placed two menus on the table, took a drink order and walked away. Tiberius looked across the table with a smug expression on his face.

"I would have thought someone in your line of work would recognise market research when you see it."

"What are you on about, Ti?"

"Consider tonight's dinner a focus group on the subject of Rachel Bailey. The only participant is Fat-Suey over there."

Jeremy attempted to stifle a laugh but failed. "What did you call her?"

"Look at her JP. With those chop sticks in her hair. What's that look? Geisha chic?"

"Not nice Tiberius."

"I'm just making a casual observation. Anyway our game plan tonight is to find out as much as possible about your new product before it's put on the market."

Jeremy sighed. "Your metaphors need some work, Ti. And how exactly do we go about this investigation?"

"It's all about subtle interrogation and observation my friend."

"Subtlety is not your strong suit. As for observation, however, I suppose your history as a peeping tom at school does qualify you for that task."

Tiberius sucked his teeth. "If Mrs. Griffith didn't want me to peep, she would have sat more lady-like in Physics class. Anyway, my theory is Fat-Suey must have seen us talking to Rachel at the bar last night. I'm sure she's curious about us. She'll want to talk."

"You've really thought this through."

"Yup. And here comes our focus group participant."

Susan returned with two Heinekens. "Have you decided what you're having?"

Tiberius reverted to his practiced formality. "We certainly have, Susan. We will both have the Outfield Burger - mine with fries, his with tossed salad."

"How would you like your burgers?"

Jeremy answered, "I'll have mine medium well. This animal will probably have his raw."

Tiberius interjected quickly, "Please ignore my less civilised friend, Susan. I'll take my burger medium, please."

The waitress smiled. "Okay, I'll be back with your order in a few minutes."

"Thank you Susan," Tiberius said, keeping the charm on high volume. "By the way, I detect a slight accent. Is that St. Lucia I'm hearing?"

"That's pretty good. I left St. Lucia as a child. Most of my family is still there though."

"I thought as much. And forgive me for my rudeness. I'm Curt and this is Jeremy."

The waitress said '*hello*' and Jeremy waved.

"I saw you guys last night sitting at the bar. Can I assume I'll be seeing a lot of you while I'm working here?"

Tiberius answered, "You certainly will. This is like our second home and our first kitchen."

Susan laughed. "I think you met a friend of mine last night. Rachel."

Tiberius furrowed his brow and scratched his cheek. "Rachel..."

Jeremy, who had so far been an extra with minimal lines in his friend's performance, jumped in.

"I think Rachel was the young lady at the bar last night chatting with Doc."

Tiberius snapped his fingers with feigned recollection. "Right! Rachel, I remember her. Seemed like a really nice girl. It makes sense that you two are friends."

Susan tilted her head and squinted a little. "How so?"

Tiberius sat back and looked directly into the waitress' eyes. "In my experience, attractive, interesting ladies tend to travel in packs."

Susan smiled shyly and looked towards the floor. "Whatever. I'm going to take care of my other customers." She looked quickly from one man to the other before walking away.

Tiberius raised his drink to his lips, but the bottle could not hide the satisfied look on his face. He took a few large gulps of his Heineken before asking, "What have we learnt so far, grasshopper?"

"Other than you being a suspiciously good actor?"

"Nothing suspicious about it, I'm a rare talent. But more importantly we learnt that if Fat-Suey is actually involved with your red-skin friend, she isn't exclusively into the fairer sex."

"And you know this because…"

"She was responding to my attention wasn't she?"

Jeremy sighed. "She was responding to something. But it could have been an upset stomach or maybe she had a headache."

"Don't be hating on a brother. Anyway, with this new information I can now proceed to use my masculine wiles to pry some information about Rachel out of her."

"I'm not sure this *'market research'* is necessary, Ti. I think I'll be fine."

"Don't be silly. This isn't really about you. It's totally about me entertaining myself at your expense."

Jeremy shook his head. "As always. Would it be too much to ask you to just leave me out of your games?"

"Come on, buddy. You know you like it." Tiberius peered over Jeremy's shoulder at the approaching waitress. "Now put on your game face 'cause act two starts… now!"

By the time they finished dinner just over an hour later, Jeremy had grudgingly accepted that Tiberius was an excellent researcher.

He was able to elicit information from the waitress seemingly at will. And at no time did she seem to realise she was being interrogated. Susan genuinely seemed to be enjoying the attention and was quite at ease chatting with her new customers.

Jeremy started his second after-dinner drink and leaned back in the booth.

"You know Tiberius, that was actually scary. I don't think I've noticed this level of manipulative behaviour from you before. Makes me wonder how much of the trouble we've gotten ourselves into over years was due to you using some sort of *Jedi* mind trick on me."

"Come on buddy, don't sell yourself short. You've always been a fantastic trouble magnet all on your own. Well, you plus alcohol."

"Whatever dude. Now, as you would say: what have we learnt?"

"Let's summarise." Tiberius leaned forward and started counting off points on his fingers. "Fat-Suey used to be a waitress at the Cloverleaf Lounge and that's where she met Rachel years ago. They've become really good friends but no confirmation yet on the nature of that friendship. They're both apparently single and neither of them have a lot of friends. And unless she's an even better actor than me, she doesn't know that you and Rachel have a date tomorrow."

Jeremy nodded. "That's about it. Plus she volunteered that she is off on Thursday night. I think you're supposed to do something with that information."

Tiberius sat back and turned his head towards the bar area where Susan was filling a drinks order.

"Nah, I'll pass. She's not really my type, and my stable is kinda full right now."

"That's never stopped you before. You've been known to keep a well packed stable with surplus on the roof."

"Guilty as charged. By the way, have I mentioned Fiona to you? I can definitely see her as my next ex-wife. She does this thing with her... oh look here comes Fat-Suey."

Susan appeared at the table with a smile. "Can I get you guys anything else from the bar?"

Tiberius looked at his watch. "No, I think that's it for the night, Susan. Just the bill, please."

The waitress looked slightly disappointed.

"But it's so early and this table has been the only one I enjoyed serving tonight. Are you sure I can't persuade you to stay a bit longer?" The last sentence was punctuated with a hand on her hip.

Tiberius smiled sweetly. "Normally we would, but we both have to work early tomorrow. I'm sure we'll run into each other here again"

Susan let out an exaggerated sigh before heading in the direction of the bar.

Jeremy looked at Tiberius. "I think she likes you, Ti."

"What's not to like? Anyway I was telling you about Fiona..."

Chapter 5

West Indies vs Pakistan
Galle, Sri Lanka

Day 3 Report
The Sri Lankan top order continued the fight back started
by their bowlers, scoring 240 runs in the day
to finish on 343-3.

Wicket-keeper batsman Kumar Sangakkara, scored an
unbeaten 126, his second Test century. This
young man is at the start of a hugely
promising career and there is great
anticipation about his future.

Thursday, November 15th, 2001

Jeremy was experiencing a singularly unproductive day at the office. In fact, if he was honest with himself, he had not completed a single significant work-related task since the Olympio presentation the previous day. Since then, it was all about anticipation.

He leaned back in his office chair and checked his watch: seventeen past eleven. Could this day go any slower?

The budget spreadsheet displayed on his computer monitor suddenly transformed into a bright blue tropical fish swimming in an aquarium, which meant that he hadn't touched the keyboard or mouse for twenty minutes.

Jeremy sighed and shifted the mouse. The spreadsheet reappeared. The budget was still incomplete. Jeremy still had nothing to add to it.

He swivelled his chair to look outside. It was a spectacularly beautiful day, but he had been so wrapped up in his thoughts all morning that he hadn't noticed. His neighbour across the street was in her usual position, engrossed in her television soap opera.

Jeremy closed his eyes and pinched the bridge of his nose.

Threesome.

He smiled and whispered the word.

"Threesome".

How could such an innocuous word create such a feeling of delicious anticipation?

He saw himself as being quite open-minded and liberal. At thirty-two years old and considered good-looking by most, he had experienced his fair share of exciting sexual encounters. One night stands during his university years seemed almost like a required course.

When he entered the working world, Jeremy became more confident and adventurous. Locations became inspired: offices; gardens; park benches; parked cars; one moving car; one airport bathroom to name a few. Light spanking, lighter bondage and various toys had all been a part of his journey. But sex with two women simultaneously remained an undiscovered country.

The adventure continued in the four years he had known Rachel. She was the most exciting woman he had ever met — in and out of bed. In many ways they had similar sexual histories and appetites. In other ways his wife was clearly the more adventurous.

Rachel had admitted to him on their first date that she had had a few dalliances with women. She never saw herself as gay or even bisexual, but instead considered being with another woman as something different, something kinky. Her first few experiences with women had been during threesomes.

Threesome.

If all went according to plan, tonight he would finally experience his first.

Rachel had earlier arranged for Susan to come over at seven o'clock that evening for a home cooked dinner. Jeremy had already worked out that dessert and coffee would be finished by eight thirty and then…

Threesome.

Jeremy glanced at his watch again: twenty-one minutes past eleven. He groaned and then leaped out of his chair, grabbed his cell phone and headed for the door. He told the nearest admin assistant that he was taking an early lunch.

He ended up on the South coast at Barbecue Barn - one of a chain of relatively low cost grill houses — and bought a fish platter to take away.

He walked back to his car which was parked across the street from the restaurant, on the periphery of the startlingly blue Caribbean Sea. It was now just after midday and with the sun at its highest, the white-sand beach was moderately filled with vacationing visitors, interspersed with the occasional local.

Jeremy took in the scene while he picked at his meal. He made it last a little under an hour while he gradually cleared his mind of his evening plans. It was the most relaxed he would be all day.

After his extended lunch break he returned to the office and was finally productive.

He finished the budget details of a new toothpaste campaign which formed part of a proposal on which he was working. He then visited his creative team and looked at some print advertising concepts for the campaign and chose two of the five for the proposal. He ended his work day with an unscheduled one-hour meeting with Martin Chandler on the subject of new business opportunities.

Jeremy left the office just after five.

While he was stuck in the evening rush hour traffic, he slipped in a CD of his favourite songs.

As he listened to the familiar opening musical cues of Marvin Gaye's '*Let's Get It On*' the feeling of anticipation rushed back all at once.

Threesome.

Susan was late and Rachel was pouting. Jeremy, as usual, was just playing it cool.

It was around twenty minutes past seven and Rachel was checking her watch for the umpteenth time since seven o'clock.

She got up from the sofa to gaze through the living room window for a moment — also for the umpteenth time — before heading to the dining room to adjust the already immaculate dinner settings.

Jeremy remained on the living room sofa watching the local news.

On the one hand he was mildly amused to see that his usually unflappable wife was capable of the occasional flap. But on the other hand, he was a little concerned that her current mood would affect the evening's plans. The other hand was gaining ascendency in Jeremy's mind.

"Don't pout, honey. I'm sure she'll be here any minute now."

Rachel glanced up sharply from the fork she was placing in the exact position it had been moments before. "I'm not pouting, Jeremy Phillips. I'm just hungry."

Jeremy was about to make a suggestive response when he heard the sound of a vehicle engine which was followed by a dance of headlights shining through the living room window.

Rachel showed little outward reaction as she shifted a wine glass in the table setting. "Please open for our guest, Jeremy," she said coolly.

Jeremy did as he was told, waiting in the doorway as Susan stepped out of her SUV. She was bathed in the glow of the nearest motion detector light, so Jeremy's first look at her in four years was properly documented.

Susan could no longer be legitimately called *Fat*-Suey.

She had lost at least twenty-five pounds since he had last seen her and was also quite toned. A tight green cotton dress clung to every curve, accentuating her new physique.

Her hair was straightened and worn open to her shoulders in what he thought of as the Cleopatra style. She looked as Rachel had described her the previous day: *hot*.

Jeremy thought that Tiberius might regret how he treated her four years before.

"Jeremy! You're looking great. Marriage clearly agrees with you," Susan said as she approached the door. She gave Jeremy a peck on his cheek.

"Thank you Susan, come on in. You're looking fantastic yourself. And that colour looks amazing on you," was all Jeremy could offer.

"Thank you Jeremy." Susan stepped past Jeremy into the living room where Rachel was waiting with arms folded across her chest.

"I see your sense of time hasn't improved with time, Susan Farrell."

Susan walked towards Rachel. "Oh quit pouting. You'll get wrinkles."

"I am not…" Rachel began before she was cut off by Susan's kiss.

Susan was wearing heels but she still stood on her toes and pressed her body firmly against Rachel's while curling her left arm around the small of his wife's back, pulling her. Her right had grabbed the back of Rachel's neck. The kiss was deep and accompanied by a sensuous moan from Susan.

Rachel kept her arms folded and body stiffened for a moment before relaxing and wrapping her arms around Susan. She returned the kiss. And the moan.

Jeremy watched from six feet away. He slowly turned and closed the front door, making as little sound as possible in an attempt to prevent any distractions from the current mood.

He walked casually to the sofa and watched, becoming more and more aroused by the moment. He hoped his extreme anticipation was not too evident.

Threesome.

The girls continued for another few seconds before Rachel pulled her head away. "You really have a way with no words, Susan."

Susan giggled. "I missed that wit. And I missed you." She gazed upwards into Rachel's eyes.

Rachel looked towards the sofa, and met Jeremy's eyes. "Should we have dinner now, or..." she began, before noticing the apparent eagerness in his pants.

Susan was also looking at Jeremy. "I don't think he's ready for dinner," she said. She returned her gaze to Rachel and added, "But I think I'm ready to eat."

———————————————

Later Jeremy would have difficulty recalling at which point during the evening they actually had dinner, but other details he recalled vividly.

He had not realised he had a voyeuristic streak until he watched Susan go down on his wife. He noted with some fascination that Susan's technique was a little different from his own - slower but firmer with lots of finger action - but seemed to have the same ultimate result. Watching his wife climax from a woman's administrations was incredibly erotic for Jeremy.

So when they turned their attentions to him, he was so ready that he had to use some mental tricks to prevent proceedings from coming to a premature end, so to speak.

It was now just after ten and Jeremy was lying in bed next to his naked, sleeping wife, who was next to the naked, sleeping waitress. The presence of two clearly exhausted ladies in his bed was an unexpected source of pride - evidence that he had more than held his own during the evening's activities. He watched them in the moonlit bed and smiled.

Jeremy slowly rolled out of bed, trying not to disturb the pair. Rachel stirred briefly then rolled onto her side towards Susan who was backing her. He stood for a moment and watched his wife spooning another woman, before heading to the kitchen.

He grabbed a canned soda from the refrigerator and drank as he walked over to the living room window, allowing the moonlight to bathe his naked body. He started to review the evening in his mind.

It was obvious to him that Susan was still really into his wife. Their friendship had ended so abruptly and badly four years before, that he wasn't surprised that there were lingering emotional strands.

But how did Rachel feel about Susan? And why did it even matter? Was this jealousy?

He remembered Tiberius' warning from the previous day and chuckled. That's it: his friend's words were just playing with his head. Trust Tiberius to somehow impose himself on the most amazing sexual experience of Jeremy's life.

Jeremy turned his attention to Susan's vehicle parked in the driveway. It looked to be a newish Honda CRV. Was it hers? If it was, how could she afford it? What was her line of work anyway? Was she still a waitress? In fact, what did he really know about her?

He took a drag of his soda.

Why did he need to know anything more about her anyway? This was most likely a onetime thing, right?

Jeremy finished the drink, dropped the can in the garbage and headed back to the bedroom. He stood in the doorway watching the pair sleeping quietly, still in a spoon position.

He carried out a final audit of his emotions. What was he feeling right now? Was there any jealousy or concern? He was satisfied that the answer was no. In fact, as he watched them, what he felt most was aroused.

"Huh," he muttered to himself as he approached the bed, intent this time on stirring his sleeping bed mates.

Chapter 6

West Indies vs Australia
St. John's, Antigua

Day 1 Report
A remarkable display of sustained fast bowling by Jermaine Lawson put West Indies in control, dismissing Australia for a disappointing 240. The visitors still had time to strike back, limiting home team to 47 for 2 at the close.

West Indies, and Lawson in particular, proved to be surprise packages today.

Friday, May 9th, 2003

"I think it's time to end this thing we're doing with Susan," Rachel declared completely out of the blue at the start of an evening of surprises.

She was at the wheel of her brand new Land Rover Defender - a company vehicle befitting her new position as sales manager - heading towards Susan's home. It was a quarter past eight in the evening.

Rachel's arrival at home with her new wheels was the evening's first surprise. The next one was her pronouncement about their complicated relationship with Susan.

Over an eighteen month period starting with what Jeremy expected would be a onetime only deal, Susan had become a regular part of their sex life. At least a few times per month the three got together to explore the corners of the unique relationship, and each other.

For the most part, everything was relaxed and enjoyable. Their completely open relationship left absolutely no room for jealously or egos, plus the sex continued to be unselfish, inventive and amazing.

However, he had noticed that his wife had become a little introspective of late on the subject of Susan. She seemed less enthusiastic about the prospect of the liaisons, even though she never failed to throw herself completely into each meeting once they occurred. Recently though, she had occasionally found reasons to postpone or cancel some of the planned sessions.

"What's up? What are you thinking?" he asked.

"Well, here's the thing. For a while now, I've been a little uncomfortable with our situation, given her lifestyle. I know you felt that way in the beginning."

Jeremy interjected, "You're right. I did feel that way at first, but you convinced me that we needn't worry as long as we minimised our contact outside of the bedroom."

"I know I did, but of late I've been having second thoughts." Rachel sighed and continued. "It's this promotion. As sales manager, I'm now in a vulnerable position. Someone could try to use my association with a criminal against me and my workplace."

They drove in silence for a minute, before Jeremy responded.

"I get what you're saying. In fact that's exactly how I felt in the beginning. Once we discovered her deal, I thought associating with her, given my position at ACA, was a risk. Why is it different now?"

Rachel didn't respond immediately. "I guess... I'm viewing it differently now that I'm that position," she admitted reluctantly.

There was more silence as her words first filled and then dissipated from the interior of the SUV.

Rachel broke the silence. "I know it sounds like I'm being selfish..."

"It does a little," Jeremy inserted.

"...but I'm just being honest. I'm sorry I never truly put myself in your shoes and took your position seriously. I'm really sorry, but I get it now."

Jeremy paused before responding tersely. "Okay. So what are we doing now? Are we going over to her place to hook up, or are we delivering the breaking news?"

"Jeremy please don't be upset with me."

"Don't get me wrong Rachel. We're both smart enough to realise that this type of relationship was unsustainable. It's amazing that it's lasted this long, but it had to end sometime, and I have no problem with that. Given everything, I am just surprised by your reason."

"JP, I understand how you feel, and I really am sorry," she said softly. "What do you want to do?"

Jeremy mulled over the question for a while. "I guess we should let her know the situation tonight. Before we do anything."

"Are you okay with that?"

"Yeah. I think it's best."

"Okay."

They drove on in silence.

Twenty minutes later they arrived at Susan's house in Kingsland Terrace, a suburb in the South of the island.

The Kingsland area was a series of relatively new developments and featured affordable houses and land. Because of this it was inhabited primarily by persons owning or renting their first homes. The prevalence of single young adults was the reason for an ongoing joke that if you visited the area around three in the morning, you could be caught in the traffic jam of cars leaving Kingsland heading to their respective homes after the overnight hook-ups.

Rachel had called Susan's cell phone on the way there but had just gotten her voicemail. Now on location, the house was in darkness, but Susan's CRV was in the driveway.

They walked to the front door and rang the doorbell while listening for any sound of movement from within. Susan wasn't known for her punctuality, so this wasn't the first time they had arrived at her place before her. What was odd was her car being there and her not answering her cell phone.

"Well, I guess that's what spare keys are for," Rachel said as she fished a set of keys from her purse. When she looked up from her purse she saw Jeremy pushing the door gently with his forefinger. It swung open soundlessly.

The looked at each other for a beat before stepping into the darkness of the living room. Jeremy fumbled on the wall for a moment before finding a light switch. The room was suddenly bathed in light revealing the nightmare into which they had stepped.

"Oh my God," Rachel said under her breath.

Practically every piece of furniture had been upended, with the cushions from the sitting room set scattered around the room. There were at least two broken wine glasses on the floor along with an unbroken wine bottle with a pattern of red wine around it. A strangely familiar odour permeated the room.

Jeremy and Rachel were still standing just inside the doorway of the living room, but could see that the kitchen was also trashed. Cupboards were thrown open with contents spilled on the floor. The same applied to the refrigerator.

"We need to call the police," Jeremy said, reaching for his phone.

"Shouldn't we check the… room… first?" Rachel asked haltingly.

Jeremy looked at his wife, immediately understanding what she meant. "Give me the key and stay here."

Rachel handed over the keyring as Jeremy turned and stepped carefully over the living room debris on his way to the guest bedroom. He found the door, which Susan always kept locked, was open, barely hanging on broken hinges.

Without stepping inside, Jeremy peered into the room, his heart beating like a drum.

There was a treadmill in the middle facing the window, with a towel hanging from one of the handles and a pair of running shoes on the walking belt. To the right were a few piles of document boxes, most of which were lying on their sides and opened. What looked like invoices, bank statements and other documents surrounded the boxes.

On the left side of the room was an inset dresser and wardrobe. Every drawer was opened and various articles of clothing, towels and linen were strewn on the floor. Jeremy looked upwards to the storage area above the dresser. He could tell without going any further into the room that the space was empty.

"Jeremy."

He turned towards his wife's voice in the kitchen just as he recognised the house's foreign odour as one he had smelt as a child. His mind was suddenly filled with a memory of watching a pig being slaughtered when he was nine years old.

He made a quick search of the other bedroom and bathroom before heading back to kitchen, where he found his wife crouching, looking at something on the floor. There was a huge pool of what looked like more red wine. Jeremy knew it wasn't.

Rachel looked up with a questioning expression as Jeremy approached.

"I just had a quick look around, but there's no sign of Susan or anyone else." He paused before adding, "And the storage area is empty."

Rachel returned her gaze to the dark pool in front of her. "There's so much blood here but where is she?" She looked up at Jeremy. "We have to call the police."

Jeremy nodded in agreement and once again reached for his phone. His eyes never left the dark pool which, from his perspective, seemed to be emanating from his crouching wife.

Chapter 7

West Indies vs Sri Lanka
Galle, Sri Lanka

Day 4 Report
Sri Lanka's batsmen batted on remorselessly before finally declaring at 590-9, giving the spinners a chance to press for victory.

West Indies finished the day on 9-1, 133 runs behind and needing to hold on for 3 more sessions for a draw. On this lifeless pitch the West Indies should only blame themselves if they fail to salvage a draw.

Friday, November 16th, 2001

Jeremy drove to work with a smile on his face.

Sure it was Friday, which always put him in a good mood, but that wasn't the reason. The traffic was surprisingly light, but he barely noticed. The match situation in Sri Lanka wasn't too bad but this caused barely a blip on his mood radar.

Jeremy's smile, and occasional wide grin, were entirely due to the previous night's escapades with Rachel and Susan. And *Susan* was definitely how he now recalled her - she would never again be Fat-Suey in his mind.

Some of his friends, including Tiberius, had described group sexual encounters as being somewhat of a crap shoot: you never quite knew what you would get. Sometimes nervousness, bad chemistry or other types of incompatibilities got in the way of enjoyment. This was definitely not his initial experience.

Jeremy had enjoyed everything about the session. Rachel had already told him about her previous encounters with women but seeing it for himself was a whole different deal.

He enjoyed being orally administered by the two women simultaneously. He found that screwing his wife while she went down on Susan was particular electrifying. Susan sitting on his face while Rachel played cowgirl on his horse was amazing.

His mind conjured up a list with the word '*Threesome*' highlighted. He made a mental checkmark next to the word.

He was turning into ACA when his phone rang. He grinned and deliberately let it ring four times before answering.

"Good morning, this is Jeremy Phillips. How may I help you?"

"Oh cut that shite out, Phillips. How was last night?" was Tiberius' greeting.

"Last night? Hmmm. Sri Lanka made a lot of runs and we are nine for one. Chris Gayle is out but we'll probably draw the match tomorrow."

There was the briefest of pauses, then: "Screw you JP."

Jeremy erupted into laughter, which continued as he parked his car and got out.

"Okay Ti. I guess you want details."

"Of course I do. Don't I always give you the full run down of my conquests?"

"Always unsolicited information."

Tiberius sucked his teeth. "Whatever. Let's hear it, man."

"Let me call you back from my desk," Jeremy said and hung up.

He snickered to himself as he pushed through the building's front door and headed to his office. He dropped into his chair and called

Tiberius at TravelWise.

"So what were we discussing?" Jeremy asked.

"So help me God, Jeremy Phillips…"

"Okay, okay Ti," said Jeremy and then he proceeded to give Tiberius a summary of his night. Tiberius was quiet throughout - a rarity in Jeremy's experience. Then he broke his silence in a very Tiberius fashion.

"Man, piss in muh pocket."

"I'd rather not" Jeremy retorted.

"I can't believe what I'm hearing?"

"It was pretty unbelievable sex, I must say."

"No not that," Tiberius said. "I mean Fat-Suey. She's hot now?"

Jeremy rolled his eyes. "Yes Ti, she's hot as hell."

"Damn JP. I guess I should have been nicer to her back then. But you did put in a good word for me, right?"

"I assure you, Ti, you never crossed my mind at any point during the night's proceedings. I was otherwise occupied"

"Always thinking about yourself. Anyway JP, frankly, I didn't think you had it in you. I'm impressed. Forget all my warnings from yesterday."

"I already have," Jeremy replied. "I always do."

"You're spunky this morning. Clearly threesomes agree with you," Tiberius said, unknowingly mirroring Susan's comment to Jeremy about marriage.

"Thanks, I guess."

"What happened after your debauchery? Was everyone cool?"

Jeremy leaned back in his chair and looked at the ceiling. "Yeah, everyone was cool. Really cool actually."

"What do you mean?"

"It was comfortable. You know, we just chatted casually, kinda fooling around, being affectionate and stuff. I don't think anyone was self-conscious or embarrassed. It was like we'd done it all before."

"Well, technically, your two ladies have done it before. Just not with you."

"Yeah, I suppose that's true. And to be honest, they being so comfortable with each other made it easier for me, I suppose."

Jeremy paused and closed his eyes, mentally reviewing portions of the previous night. "You know, they were so comfortable, that at times it was like I was watching lesbian porn or something. Really good lesbian porn"

"Huh," Tiberius said. "My friend, you have stumbled ass-backwards into the best type of threesome: girl-girl-boy, and the girls are into each other. Jackpot!"

Jeremy turned in his chair and looked through his window. "She invited us to her place tonight for a return engagement."

"Huh," Tiberius repeated. "So soon? You're not planning on making this a regular thing, are you?"

"I haven't planned anything at all."

"Remember what I told you yesterday…"

"No, I do not," Jeremy interrupted.

"...about the dangers of reminding your lovely wife of the existence of great, exciting sex? How is she going to return to your dull, one dimensional game after this?" Tiberius asked, before chuckling for a few seconds.

"Piss off, Ti."

Jeremy swivelled in his chair again to face his desk.

"However I agree that this shouldn't be a regular thing. I barely know the girl, so who knows who she talks to. And this is Barbados. This type of stuff tends to get around and that wouldn't be good for business if you know what I mean."

"Exactly," Tiberius said. "You are both upstanding members of society. Leave that type of reputation for me. I can take it. In fact I think I'm going to start telling your story from last night as if it was mine."

Jeremy sighed. "Do whatever you want, Tiberius."

"I always do. Where does Fat-Suey live by the way?"

"I think Rachel said Kingsland. Why?"

"No reason. I am definitely *not* going to stake out her house tonight in hopes of getting a glimpse of her and Rachel in action. I am definitely *not* going to do that."

"Just remember that in order to see them, you're probably going to have to see a lot of my naked ass as well."

"Hmmm," Tiberius said with mock gravity. "Valid point. That would be horrible to see: definitely bony and probably hairy. But it might be worth it, you know. I have to weigh the pros and cons of this."

Jeremy sighed again. "Goodbye, Tiberius. I have work to do."

Jeremy hung up to peals of Tiberius' laughter. He estimated that half of their conversations ended exactly like that.

He stood up, put his hands in his pockets and looked out his window. He smiled for a moment remembering specific details of the previous night.   But he also wondered whether such an early return visit to Susan's would be setting a bad precedent.

Before his conversation with Tiberius, he hadn't given any serious thought to possible fallout. Both ACA owners were family men who tried to instil Christian principles in the running of their business. He didn't think that a senior employee living a '*deviant*' lifestyle would sit well with them.

Jeremy pondered this for a moment. The possible negatives were off-set by one simple fact: his first threesome experience was awesome and he wanted to do it again.

He sighed. Then he smiled.

Decision made. He would have only himself to blame for any repercussions from here on.

At just after six thirty that evening Jeremy and Rachel pulled up to the address in Kingsland Terrace which, according to the directions Rachel had scribbled, was Susan's house.

They sat in the car for a few moments looking at the moderately sized one-story bungalow sitting behind a classic white picket fence.

Even in the faltering light they could make out an impeccably manicured lawn, dotted with a variety of flowering plants, the centre piece being a small rock garden enveloped in a lush flowering vine. Similar vines crept up the latticework at both visible corners of the house, creating green accents against what looked like beige walls.

A short cobble stone path lead to a tiny veranda which surrounded the front door. Susan's SUV, which was parked at the end of the path, seemed almost anachronistic in the quaint setting.

Rachel said what Jeremy was thinking.

"This is a really nice place," she said, not attempting to hide the surprise in her voice.

"Where did you say she is working these days?" Jeremy asked.

"She never really said, actually. I know she's not waiting tables anymore, but somehow I got the impression she was mostly unemployed."

"Huh," said Jeremy. They looked at the house in silence for a few seconds longer before glancing at each other and simultaneously reaching for their door handles.

Susan was already at the open front door of the house when they reached it. "I thought you two weren't going to come inside. Welcome to Casa Farrell."

She stepped to one side and waved her right arm like a game show hostess to guide them inside.

Jeremy let Rachel walk ahead of him. Inside was decorated with very contemporary furniture and fixtures. The open plan living room connected to a dining room and large kitchen with a lovely polished granite island. Everything was currently enveloped in a delicious aroma of something cooking.

"You have a lovely home, Susan. That landscaping is amazing by the way," Rachel said looking around.

"Thank you. I wanted outside to look like a perfect twenty-first century cottage. That's why my landscaper is on speed dial," Susan said with a giggle. "All the houses in Kingsland look so similar: I just wanted mine to stand out."

"So this *is* your house then. Not a rental?" Rachel enquired.

"It's not a rental. You can say it was a gift from a dear friend. But a gift I earned," Susan answered vaguely. "Let me give you the grand tour."

Susan seemed to take great pride in showing the couple each room, pausing to highlight pieces of art or some new techie device. As they walked through a short corridor they passed a closed door. Susan located a key from a bunch she was carrying.

"This is my guest bedroom," she said, unlocking the door. "And since I never have guests, it's really my exercise room." She opened the door long enough to show that there was no sign of a bed, but a treadmill, yoga mat and a few free weights were in view. She then closed and locked the door.

"Next stop is my favourite room," she said with a cheeky tone, as she approached the open door of the master bedroom. Like the rest of the house it was very tastefully decorated, the highlight being a four poster bed. Susan sat on the edge of the bed, smiling while Rachel and Jeremy looked around.

"I have to agree with my wife," Jeremy admitted. "This truly is a lovely house. It would make an excellent venue to shoot some commercials actually. If you're up to it, there may be some location fees in your future."

"Why thank you, Jeremy. That's nice of you to say but I don't think I need strangers in my house." She then bounced up off the bed and headed to the door.

"So dinner isn't quite ready, but let me get you some drinks. Scotch and water for madam; Heineken in zee bottle for zee monsieur," she said, lapsing into an exaggerated French accent, while walking towards the kitchen. They followed her.

"Good memory," Jeremy acknowledged.

"Once a waitress," Susan said. Then she turned and faced them. "In fact, I have a special treat for you two this evening. To show my appreciation for a great time last night, tonight I will be your waitress. Tonight, I cater to you." The cheeky tone returned to her voice.

Rachel didn't miss a beat. She took Jeremy's hand and turned back to the master bedroom. "Well, in that case you can bring us our drinks in here. I saw an apron in the kitchen. Be sure you're wearing that and nothing else when you serve us."

Jeremy simply allowed himself to be led and a few minutes later, allowed himself to be served.

An hour later they were all sharing a bottle of red wine at the dinner table, topless with the exception of Susan who was still wearing the apron.   She had demonstrated her cooking skills with a delicious spread that included Bajan styled macaroni pie, grilled fish, garlic bread and a Greek salad.

"This must be a unique record. That's two nights in a row that we had dessert first and then a half-naked dinner," Jeremy observed slyly.

Susan blew him a kiss and said, "Well I'm not complaining and I hope you aren't either."

"I'm sure he's not," Rachel added. "He's been dreaming of this for a long, long time."

"Oh has he now?" Susan said. "So have we made your dreams come true, Jeremy?"

Jeremy sighed and pretended to be offended. "I can see I'm outnumbered here, so if you don't mind I'll just go over there and watch some TV."

He got up and headed to the living room. The girls started whistling and making kissing noises at his rear, prompting Jeremy to bend over in an exaggerated way before settling into the sofa. He switched on the television and got comfortable watching an NBA game.

"Watching TV is often a Jeremy code for taking a nap," Rachel said as she stood up and started to clear the dishes from the table.

Susan interrupted her. "No no no, Rachel. I'll take care of the dishes later. Let's go join Jeremy." She grabbed the wine bottle and headed towards the living room.

Rachel put down the plates, picked up the glasses and followed. They ended up on the carpet in front of the sofa. Glasses were distributed and Susan filled them the California red.

"This feels like we're at a slumber party," Rachel admitted. "But a naughty one. With wine. And no clothes."

Susan smiled. "Doesn't it remind you of us back in the day, Rachel?"

Rachel lowered her eyes. "I guess it does a little."

There was silence as they took sips from their glasses while Jeremy pretended to be engrossed in the game on the television. Rachel was the first to speak.

"Tell me about this house, Susan. What do you mean it was a gift?"

There was a brief hesitation before Susan answered. "It's a longish story, but i'll give you the summary. Remember my friend Barry that you met at the dealership on Wednesday? Barrington."

"Of course."

"It's his house but he's given me complete and total use of it. Free of charge."

Rachel sipped her wine. "So you two are an item then"

"Not exactly. He prefers whores actually." Rachel gave her a look. "And I am not a whore, Rachel," she added, tossing a throw pillow at her.

Rachel caught it, laughing.

"But you're involved in some way I assume."

Susan hesitated and glanced at Jeremy. Rachel read her expression.

"It's okay Susan. You can speak freely in front of JP. He's like one of the gals."

Jeremy grunted wordlessly and shifted his position on the sofa so that the semi-turgid bulge in his boxers was more prominently displayed.

The girls laughed.

"Well okay, Barry and I have been involved off and on for a couple of years, but it's nothing official," Susan revealed.

"But this house is pretty official though," Jeremy blurted. Rachel looked at him sharply.

"You're right, JP. You see, Barry and I also have a business relationship. He owns construction and landscaping businesses so this is like his dual purpose show house. I stay here to make sure the place looks lived-in and occasionally I have to give guided tours."

"Sounds like a good job if you can get it," Jeremy said.

Rachel was looking at Susan through squinted eyes. "So Susan, when we went out on Wednesday, you mentioned that you were kinda seeing someone. Was it Barry you were talking about?"

Susan grinned sheepishly. "Kinda, but I also got myself a toy boy. Wait here." She leapt off the floor and headed to the bedroom. Rachel looked at Jeremy and shrugged.

Susan quickly returned, holding a book which turned out to be a copy of Stephen King's *It*.

She opened the book and removed what looked like a piece of white card being used as a bookmark. Turning it over revealed a photograph of a young man shot from the waist up, lying shirtless in a bed. His face was framed by short dreadlocks which also accentuated piercing dark eyes that stared directly into the camera. Those eyes smouldered with an emotion that was far from happiness.

"Adrian doesn't like taking pictures so this is the only one I have. He wasn't thrilled to be on camera as you can see."

"He's a cutie, in a thuggish sort of way," Rachel said. "Looks like you're robbing the cradle though."

"Hey. He's twenty-two, okay," Susan revealed with a laugh. "That's only seven years younger than me. That's permitted isn't it?"

Jeremy was scrutinising the photograph. "He's Adrian who?"

"Barrett. Adrian Barrett," answered Susan. "He's such a sweetheart."

Jeremy turned the name around in his mind. He knew he'd seen Adrian Barrett before but couldn't place him.

"So does Adrian know about Barry?" Rachel asked.

"He does, and that's where it get tricky." Susan paused for effect. "Barry is Adrian's boss."

Rachel erupted into peals of laughter. "Susan you're such a drama whore. Couldn't you make things any more complicated?"

"I know, I know," Susan whined. "It all just sort of happened."

"I take it Barry doesn't know about Adrian, though," Jeremy posited.

"No he doesn't. And that's why I'm hiding Adrian's picture in this book," Susan explained. "Barry isn't much of a reader." She chuckled lightly.

"He might not be much of a reader, but according to Rachel he's looking at blowing half million dollars on a car," Jeremy offered. "Not bad for a non-reader."

Susan sipped her wine before responding. "I didn't mean he can't read, JP. I meant he's not much of a recreational reader. Barry has an amazing head for business, is great with people and is a really hard worker. He's done well for himself starting with nothing."

"So it would seem," Rachel agreed. "But the big question on my mind is how do JP and I fit into your complicated life?"

Susan looked from Rachel up to JP and back again. She then leaned forward and kissed Rachel on the lips. With her left hand she reached up and stroked the bulge in Jeremy's boxers. After a few seconds she pulled her lips away from Rachel.

"I think you all fit just fine."

Chapter 8

West Indies vs Australia
St. John's, Antigua

Day 2 Report
*West Indies were bowled out for 240, equalling Australia's
first innings total, before a massive unbroken opening
partnership of 171 put the visitors in command at the end
of the second day.*

*Relations between the two sides grew progressively more
hostile as the day progressed, typified by angry exchanges
between the opposing captains. One wonders what impact
the foul tempers and aggressive behaviour will have on the
rest of this match.*

Saturday, May 10th, 2003

Oistins is a coastal town located in the South of Barbados.

Originally a fishing village, the area developed into a major tourist
attraction over the years. This status had little to do with the rustic
appeal of the continued fishing trade or its proximity to the gorgeous
Miami beach. Its appeal was primarily due to the popularity of the
Friday night fish fry, which had become an essential social event for
visitors and locals alike.

Aside from thriving fish markets, the area included a shopping mall, bars, restaurants, gaming arcades, an Anglican church and a police station.

Jeremy and Rachel were sitting in the waiting area of the Oistins Police Station.

It was approaching one o'clock in the morning: more than four hours after they discovered Susan's ransacked place and that pool of blood. Three hours after police arrived on the scene. Two hours after they came to the station. One hour after they made their written statements, completed longhand and in triplicate.

They were waiting to be interviewed by a detective who had apparently not yet returned from the crime scene. Since then, they were essentially ignored and as the shock of the night's events started to wear off, their mood was heading towards foul.

Several times Jeremy approached the nearest duty officer sitting behind a counter to ask for an update. Each time, he was told that someone would be with them very soon.

They continued to sit on the uncomfortable bench sipping watery, lukewarm coffee. The distinctive sounds of Karaoke originating from the nearby fish fry did nothing to improve their worsening moods.

Eventually the duty officer called the couple and escorted them into an interrogation room. This was Jeremy's first visit to a police station and his expectations for an interrogation room were based on what he had seen on television shows.

What he found was a small office, sparsely decorated with a rusting metal desk, a matching credenza, plastic chairs and a standing fan rotating in the corner. There were no hot lamps, two-way mirrors or obvious recording devices.

Sitting behind the desk, scribbling on a yellow legal pad was a slim, dark skinned man who looked like could be in his early forties. His hair and facial hair were speckled grey, which almost matched the frames of his full rimmed glasses.

He stood and gestured for them to sit on the opposite side of the desk, revealing crisp, beige slacks which complemented his blue and white striped, button down shirt.

"Mr. and Mrs. Phillips, I am Detective Harold Mason. Sorry about the long wait but as you can imagine this is an abnormal situation."

They sat without responding. A uniformed policeman entered, closing the door behind him.

"This is Constable Mark D'Hayle. He'll be joining us for this interview," Mason explained.

The constable looked to be in his mid-twenties, tall and well built. He nodded at the couple as he passed them before assuming a position leaning on the wall behind Mason.

The detective shuffled sheets of paper together and laid them on the desk next to the legal pad.

"I read your statements and just want to fill in some blanks. First, how do you know Miss Farrell?"

Jeremy looked at Rachel as she answered. "She's my friend really. We met eight or nine years ago and we've been friends on and off since then."

"What does on and off mean?"

Rachel looked slightly exasperated. "We were friends and then we weren't for a while. Then two years ago we met again and have been friends since then."

Mason scribbled something on the legal pad. "According to your statement you have keys to her house. That would suggest you are quite close."

Rachel narrowed her eyes. "It would suggest that, wouldn't it," she said tersely.

Mason met her gaze for a few moments before continuing. "Are you aware that the house isn't hers at all?"

Jeremy chimed in. "Yes, we are aware. She told us it belongs to her boss. It's a show house which she manages for him."

Mason glanced at Jeremy without moving his head. "So you'll understand why we're surprised that you have keys to that house."

The couple looked back at Mason silently.

The detective glanced down at his notes before continuing. "Anyway, you mentioned her boss. Do you know who that is?"

"She worked for a company called Absolute Shore-ity," Rachel responded.

Mason looked up at Rachel. "I notice you said 'worked'. Does she no longer work there or do you have reason to believe she's dead?"

Rachel was caught off guard by the question. "I don't know… all that blood…" she stammered.

Jeremy interrupted. "We don't know whether she's dead or not, okay? In fact, do you even know for sure that the blood is hers?"

Mason raised an eyebrow. "That's a valid query Mr. Phillips. We're comparing DNA in the blood with hair and other materials we found at the scene. Unfortunately, the lab is in Trinidad, so we may not have any results for up to ten days, depending on workload."

"I see," Jeremy muttered.

Mason looked at the two of them for a few seconds before continuing.

"You mentioned Absolute Shore-ity. What do you know about that company?"

Jeremy answered. "As far as I know it's a construction and landscaping group, detective. But why are you asking us these questions?"

"As I said, we're filling in blanks. Please bear with us. Do you know the owner of this company?"

Jeremy looked at Rachel before answering. "I think his name is Barry Shorey. Susan has mentioned him a few times."

"So you don't associate with him? He's not a friend?"

"Not at all," said Jeremy.

"Even though you have keys to a house he owns. Actually more than a house, an important part of his business: a show house."

Rachel looked annoyed. "As we said, Susan gave us some spare keys. She travels often so she asks me to clear her mailbox and stuff for her. Plus, you know, in case she locks herself out or something."

"Oh I get that. You give spares to your most trusted friends. I do it as well."

Mason turned to a previous page in the legal pad. "Where do you work, Mrs. Phillips?"

"Warrens Motors."

"What do you do there?"

"I'm a sales manager."

"Were you a sales manager on…" he referred to his notes. "… December 10th, 2001?

"No. I was a sales executive back then."

"So you may or may not have been aware that on that date Mr. Shorey took delivery of a 2002 Range Rover Sport, valued at…," Mason glanced at his notes again. "… $470,000."

The colour drained from Rachel's face. She opened her mouth to respond and then closed it. Jeremy placed his hand on her knee and squeezed reassuringly.

"I… I sold it to him," Rachel haltingly confessed.

There was no surprise on the detective's face. "Is that so? Yet a moment ago when I asked about Barrington Shorey, who you guys call Barry it would seem, you didn't seem to know much about him."

Rachel started to regain her composure. "It simply slipped my mind."

"Did it?" Mason asked looking at Rachel. "Well, it was just one encounter two years ago, so that's understandable. It *was* one encounter on December 10th, 2001 and that's it, right?"

Rachel looked down at her knees and sighed. "He would have come in a month or so previously and we spoke and met a few times before the sale was confirmed."

Mason leaned back in his chair and looked at Rachel. D'Hayle shifted his position on the wall.

Rachel continued. "I know how it sounds, but I just didn't think of that business interaction when you asked if we associated with him. And he definitely isn't a friend. We referred to him as Barry because that's what Susan called him. Calls him."

Jeremy interrupted once more. "Detective, are my wife and I being investigated for something? Are we being arrested or charged?"

Mason was still leaning back in his chair. "Mr. Phillips, a serious crime has apparently been committed. At this moment we don't know if it's an abduction, something worse or nothing at all. The information you provide is essential for understanding the circumstances that led to where we are right now. I know it's late and you've had a long night, but the more you cooperate, the sooner we can be done here."

Jeremy looked at his wife who was once again looking at her knees. "Okay. What else do you want to know?"

Mason leaned forward and referred to his notes. "Mrs. Phillips, do you remember how Mr. Shorey paid for his vehicle two years ago?"

Rachel looked at the detective. "What do you mean?"

"I mean how was it financed? Did he get a loan? Did he write a cheque? Did he walk in with a big bag of cash? That last one would be memorable."

Rachel ran her fingers through her hair. "I don't remember. Most transactions in that price range are businesses leases, often duty free. Occasionally a high net worth individual will simply write a cheque. Loans are less common but they happen occasionally."

Mason was scribbling in his legal pad. "That was informative. Would it surprise you to learn that Mr. Shorey wrote a cheque for his purchase, duty paid?"

"In my line of work, I have learnt not to prequalify anyone's ability to afford a vehicle. We sell the car and the accounts department deals with the financial aspects."

"So you're not surprised."

"No I am not," Rachel snapped.

Mason raised his hand with the palm facing Rachel. "Take it easy Mrs. Phillips. Let's move on. You mentioned that Miss Farrell travels often. Is this for business or pleasure?"

"Both I guess. She said her boss sometimes asks her do errands for him throughout the Caribbean and she takes advantage of these trips to take short vacations."

"What type of errands?"

"I never asked."

"Hmmm," Mason said referring to his notes. "You mentioned that Miss Farrell manages the show house for Mr. Shorey. Is that a paying job?"

"As far as I know."

"And that's her only occupation?"

"To my knowledge."

"From what you saw tonight, was there anything missing from the house?"

Jeremy looked over to his wife, who appeared deep in thought. After a few moments she responded. "Nothing obvious. I didn't notice anything."

The detective shifted his gaze to Jeremy who shrugged. "No idea."

Mason read through his notes in silence for a while. "Finally, do you know anyone that would want to hurt Miss Farrell for any reason?"

Rachel paused for a few moments before saying she didn't.

"Thank you for your patience Mr. and Mrs. Phillips. We are treating this as a serious crime. It's an active investigation so we will probably have to be in touch again."

The couple stood to leave. Mason also got to his feet.

"If you think of anything useful at any time you should immediately call the station."

He produced a business card from his breast pocket and held it towards the couple. "Or you can call me directly. My mobile number is right there."

Jeremy took the card and they turned towards the door.

"One other thing before you go," Mason said. "Whether you actually know him well or not, Barrington Shorey is certainly well known to the force, along with a number of his associates. He is not a man to be trifled with. I would be very careful if were you." He then added in a softer tone, "But I am here to help."

They absorbed his comments and left the station.

After a wordless drive home, Jeremy and Rachel shared a silent shower before turning in.

Sleep proved impossible.

They each lay in bed - Rachel on her side and Jeremy on his back - staring into the nothingness of the darkened room.

After a futile half hour, Jeremy gingerly got up and left the bedroom, returning a few minutes later with a half filled brandy snifter. He adopted a seated position in bed, took a sip while caressing Rachel's hair. She turned at his touch and the smell of brandy, sat up and accepted the drink her husband was now dangling in front of her nose. She sipped deeply and exhaled.

"JP, are we in trouble?"

Jeremy drank before responding. "I don't think so. We haven't done anything wrong."

"But we know what's been going on. We know what's missing. And we know who took Susan, don't we?" She paused. "Or killed her."

Jeremy pulled Rachel towards him so her head was on his chest. He stroked her hair. "Do we really know who's responsible?"

"It's got to be Barry, right?"

"We don't know that for sure. In his business he must have enemies."

"So I ask again, are we in trouble?"

Jeremy considered the question for a few moments.

"I'm sure we'll be fine," he said to his wife as well as to himself.

They finished the drink in silence.

Sleep came, but rest didn't. They eventually rose after ten o'clock but then proceeded to spend most of Saturday in bed.

They kept waiting for some type of update on the case from Detective Mason, but none came.

Occasionally Rachel dialled Susan's cell phone number, but the calls went to voice mail each time.

By the time the local news aired at seven o'clock that night, Susan's disappearance was the lead-off story.

Chapter 9

West Indies vs Pakistan
Peshawar, Pakistan

Day 3 Report
West Indies face an uphill task to avoid defeat after trailing by 230 on the first innings, and losing 2 early wickets on reaching 99 at the end of the third day.

Leg spinner Rawle Lewis proved to be mostly ineffective, experiencing a real baptism of fire in a forgettable international debut.

Wednesday, November 19th, 1997

Kendal Sporting was a shooting range and country club, located in the South East parish of St. Philip.

Its setting was a remodelled plantation house and featured a picturesque clubhouse with a restaurant and swimming pool. There was also an extensive lake which allowed members to try their hands at sport fishing.

But Kendal was mostly about shooting - pistol, shotgun, paintball and archery. There were two pistol ranges: one outdoor and one indoor with seven shooting bays.

Jeremy and Tiberius were in the indoor range practicing with Glock 27 pistols.   It was approaching midday and as they did most Wednesday, the guys were having a short competitive shooting session before lunch.

Tiberius was practically a savant with any type of gun. He was good enough to have won many local competitions but as with many areas in his life, simply wasn't interested enough to take his skills any further.

Jeremy was competent with the handgun. He tried to take shooting seriously but was unable to compete at Tiberius' level, even when the latter wasn't trying very hard. Today was no different.

After their half hour session, they headed to the clubhouse for their pre-ordered lunch. Jeremy had a club sandwich while Tiberius chose a burger topped with blue cheese.

After the typically delicious meal, they headed back to their respective workplaces in Tiberius' fully pimped out Mazda Lantis, listening to the radio through ridiculously expensive Blaupunkt speakers.

When the first few notes of *Hypnotize* by The Notorious B.I.G. burst crisply out of the sound system, Tiberius turned up the volume and rapped along. Jeremy supported him with the occasional Puff Daddy-style '*huh*' on the beats. When the song reached the chorus they belted out the lyrics in unison.

"Oh yeah, dude, that could be my theme song," Tiberius said as the radio DJ's voice signalled the end of the track. "Puts me in the mood to do something later. What are you up to?"

"Remember, I've got a date."

"Oh right. The fair Rachel Bailey. Are you ready?"

"Of course. Why shouldn't I be?"

"Well, as I said before, she's insanely hot. I mean, you've inexplicably had your share of good looking chicks over the years, but this one is in a different league."

"She's no hotter than Kaye Bishop or Debra Yearwood."

"First of all, both of those were university pussy, which doesn't count. Secondly, neither Kaye nor Debra were bedtime all-rounders, as far as I know anyway. With Rachel, you have the chance to open your orgy account - if you don't mess up tonight that is. No pressure." Tiberius laughed at his own joke.

"Even with all of your twisted research last night, we haven't actually confirmed that Rachel and Susan are involved. And I'm not sure we can take Doc's words as gospel. He might have been trying to scare us off so he could make his own moves," Jeremy reasoned.

"True, true," Tiberius agreed. "I guess it's up to you to do the definitive research while you're getting all up in it."

"That's not my plan for tonight at all. I'm just going to have a few drinks with a smoking hot chick. As you said, no pressure. I'm not you."

"That's right my friend, you're not me. *Guess that's why you stroke and I get laid*," he sang, butchering The Notorious B.I.G.'s lyrics.

He broke into a full Tiberius laughter spell.

Jeremy joined him. He had to admit it was pretty funny even if it was at his expense.

Jeremy arrived at the Cloverleaf Lounge just before seven that evening. He sat at the bar, ordered a Heineken and looked around.

Cloverleaf could fairly be described as primarily a gaming arcade but with a decent bar and restaurant attached.

From where he sat, he could see maybe thirty persons spread throughout the banks of slot machines which took up about sixty percent of the floor space. At the same time, only two of the sixteen booths in the dining area were occupied and there was one person at the bar other than Jeremy.

He had met her only once and with alcohol in the mix, so Jeremy had started to doubt whether Rachel Bailey was as beautiful as he remembered. He was quickly disavowed of that notion when she entered the Cloverleaf a few minutes after him.

Despite a simple beige skirt-suit with brown heels, there seemed to be a lull in the ambient sounds of conversation and musical chimes from the slot machines in her wake.

She was raking her fingers through her short, brown hair as she caught sight of Jeremy and vectored towards the bar.

He stood as she approached, almost at a loss for words. "Hi Rachel," he said mildly.

"Hello Jeremy-Phillips-from-last-night-at-the-Outfield. Are we sitting at the bar or should we go to a booth?"

Jeremy smiled. "Sounds like you want to go to a booth."

"Well, it's more private and who knows, drinks might turn into dinner if things go well."

"I love a woman that thinks ahead," Jeremy said, instantly regretting throwing around the 'L' word so liberally.

He motioned to the bartender that he was moving to a booth, before allowing Rachel to choose one. They settled into one that was far enough from the sounds of the slot machines to make for a comfortable conversational volume.

"Sorry, I didn't have a chance to go home first. I had a long day at work and by the time I was finished I didn't see the point of heading all the way home to come back out," Rachel volunteered.

"Where's home for you?"

"I'm from Guinea, St. John."

St. John was a rustic parish on the eastern side of the island.

"Wow, that's quite a commute. I can understand why you didn't go home."

A waiter came over, took a drink order from Rachel and left two menus on the table.

"So what's a long day at work like for you?" Jeremy asked.

"Well I'm a sales exec…"

"Senior sales executive if I remember correctly," interrupted Jeremy.

Rachel smiled. "That's right. Which makes me kinda like a brand manager without the title. So I deal not just with my own sales, but any sales involving my brand, which is Land Rover."

"Sounds fancy."

"It's not really," said Rachel with a laugh. "It's hard work. The people that can afford to buy those vehicles in Barbados have to be treated a certain way."

"What do you mean?"

"Take today for example. I'm dealing with a British gentleman who owns a home here and spends a few months a year in the island. He wants a blue Range Rover but wanted to make sure that it could be driven comfortably to all the places he normally frequents in Barbados. Well miracle of miracles, we happen to have a blue one in stock, so off we go on a test drive to his house and then to seven different locations. I had to smile and put up with his clumsy flirting for almost three hours."

"That really was a rough day."

"That actually isn't the worst of it. His bellman, who is responsible for managing the house when the owner isn't here, apparently told him he doesn't like the blue colour, and that silver would be a better choice for the tropics. Bloody hell! So now after piling up three hours worth of mileage on one car that is actually here, I had to order a silver one, which will take another five months to arrive."

"At least you got a sale out of it, right?"

"Yes I did. I mean, I did smile and put up with his passes for three hours didn't I?" Rachel said with a giggle.

"I suppose you did. But one thing I have to say about all of that."

"What?"

"Silver really is a better colour for the tropics."

"Frig you. Who asked you anyway?" They both laughed as the waiter returned with Rachel's whiskey and water.

"Are you ready to order?" he asked.

Jeremy responded somewhat sheepishly. "We haven't even looked at the menu. We'll call you over when we're ready."

Rachel's phone vibrated in her purse. She fished it out, glanced at the caller ID then replaced it without answering.

"What about you? What do you do other than try to pick up strange women in bars?" she asked.

"You're saying you're strange?"

"You're saying you were trying to pick me up?"

Jeremy grimaced. "Ouch. Touché. You win. I'll move on."

Rachel laughed as Jeremy continued. "I'm an account executive at

ACA - a marketing firm."

"I've heard of it. You guys did some work for that big polo tournament at Holder's last year."

Jeremy nodded. "The Holder's Polo International. We handled the marketing and event management."

"I remember. That was well done. We were a sponsor and had some cars on display there but I don't remember seeing you."

"I was only there for a short time each day to make sure everything was set up properly. Polo really isn't my game."

"What is your game?"

"I like cricket. Passionate about it actually."

"Ooh. Passion is so rare in men," Rachel said seductively.

Jeremy smiled. Before he could respond, Rachel's phone vibrated again. As before she glanced at it but didn't answer.

"Is everything all right?" Jeremy asked.

"Yes. You were telling me about your passion… for cricket."

"Are you a fan?" Jeremy asked.

"Not really, but based on the talk at work today the West Indies are playing Pakistan right now and they aren't doing so well."

"Correct. When I was introduced to cricket by my father at ten years old, West Indies were the best, most exciting team in the world. My dad used to take me to games and explain all the rules and nuances. I've been hooked ever since. Right now the West Indies are on a bit of a decline but I never lost that passion for the team or the game."

"Wow, that's wonderful. Are you still close with your dad?"

"He died about five years ago. My mom passed last year. But we were always close."

"Sorry to hear," Rachel said solemnly. "My mom died when I was five. I never knew my father. I was raised mostly by my grandmother who is now eighty-four but thinks she's forty-eight."

Jeremy laughed. "So we're both orphans then. Let's drink to that."

They raised their drinks and each took a sip. Then Rachel's phone vibrated once more. She sighed.

"I am so sorry about this. Let me take this call." She grabbed her bag, slid out of the booth and headed outside.

Jeremy called over the waiter and ordered some more drinks. He finished off the first Heineken while he waited for Rachel. She returned after a few minutes looking annoyed. She tossed back the rest of her drink as soon as she sat down.

"We need more drinks," she said evenly.

"I just ordered. What's up? You seem upset."

Rachel didn't respond immediately. She closed her eyes, took a deep breath, exhaled slowly before reopening her eyes and fixing them on Jeremy.

"It's a first date Jeremy. I don't want to be a downer."

"It's okay Rachel. I'm a good listener."

Rachel forced a smile. "Alright. I have a friend who's a little upset that I'm on a date. Actually livid would be a better word."

"Oh ho," said Jeremy. "Boyfriend? Ex-boyfriend?"

"Nothing like that. It's just a casual thing with a long time friend. But it seems…" Rachel hesitated. "It seems… she is taking things more seriously than I am."

Rachel looked directly into Jeremy's eyes as she uttered the last sentence. Jeremy didn't break eye contact.

He asked, "Well, how do you feel about her?"

The waiter returned with the drinks. Rachel maintained eye contact with Jeremy throughout. She took a sip of the new drink in this manner.

"For me it's been fun, just a little diversion. She's a great friend but not really my type for a relationship of any substance. Not that I've ever been in a serious relationship with a girl."

"But you have been with girls before this one."

Rachel laughed. "Jeremy Phillips, how did we get here? I don't even know why I'm telling you any of this."

Jeremy smiled. "It's because I have a trustworthy way about me. Plus we're orphan buddies now. We drank on it."

Rachel laughed again. "You have a point. Anyway, you're right. I have been with a few girls before. Just for fun, you know, kicks."

"So would you consider yourself bisexual?"

Rachel shook her head vigorously. "Not at all. Most of my encounters with girls have been when me and a guy I'm dating have had threesomes. There have been a few exception, maybe three times that I've been one on one with a girl."

"Some people would say that's plenty."

Rachel smiled. "Are you one of those people?"

"Nope. I believe once we accept that sex is about something other than procreation, then we accept that it's about pleasure. If it's about pleasure then whatever pleases you should be fine."

Rachel looked directly into Jeremy's eyes again. Then she smiled again.

"Jeremy Phillips you are quite a surprise."

She took another sip of her drink.

"Anyway let me be clear. I am not particularly attracted to women per se, and as I said before, I can't conceive of being in a serious relationship with one." She paused and leaned forward in her seat. "For me, being with a woman is something kinky. Something to spice things up. But that's it."

"So what you're saying is you're a fan of the dick, then."

Rachel laughed. "Oh I'm a big fan of the dick. In fact I'm a fan of the big dick," she said with a wink.

It was Jeremy's turn to laugh. Rachel's phone buzzed again. She ignored it.

"So what's the deal with that girl then?" Jeremy asked indicating the phone in her bag with a motion of his head. "Is *she* gay?"

Rachel shook her head slowly. "Susan says I'm the first woman she's been with. I guess that why she's all caught up. Oh that's her name by the way - Susan. In fact you may have seen her. She works at the Outfield. She was there on Monday night."

"Oh right. I did meet her. Actually she was Tiberius' and my waitress last night." Jeremy paused before adding, "Tiberius calls her Fat-Suey."

Rachel looked genuinely horrified, "Oh my God, that's awful. He didn't say it to her face did he?"

"No. Just to me."

"Still awful."

"Tiberius can be pretty bad."

"Clearly. Wait. Was it because she was wearing those chop sticks in her hair?"

"Something like that."

Rachel sighed exaggeratedly. "Well, I can see why he called her that. But still, that's not very nice."

They smiled at each other.

The phone vibrated.

Rachel exhaled sharply. "Jeremy I am really sorry, but I think I have a situation to deal with. Would it be terrible of me to take off now?"

"I'll be disappointed but I understand you have a task at hand. Hopefully I'll have other opportunities to impress you with my charm and wit."

Rachel slid across to Jeremy and pecked him on his cheek. "You're sweet. I'll make sure you have plenty of opportunities to impress me," she whispered before sliding out of the booth and out the door.

Jeremy continued to sip his drink in silence.

The waiter came over to clear Rachel's glass.

"Will you be having anything else?"

Jeremy opened one of the menus. "Buddy, things went well so I'll have some dinner," he said to the very confused waiter.

Chapter 10

West Indies vs Australia
St. John's, Antigua

Day 3 Report
Matthew Hayden hammered a magnificent 177 as Australia
compiled 417 in their second innings. By the close of play,
the West Indies openers had nibbled 47 runs out of the
unlikely target of 418.

With 2 whole days left in the game, West Indies will need to
put on an amazing batting display to avoid defeat or reach
a world record score to win.

Sunday, May 11th, 2003

After the Friday night / Saturday morning ordeal at Susan's home and the police station, Jeremy and Rachel finally had a restful night and woke up on Sunday morning feeling refreshed.

They got out of bed just after seven and decided to go for a jog through their neighbourhood returning an hour later, showered and prepared breakfast together.

After the meal they lounged in the living room and watched a movie on HBO.

While watching, Rachel removed the polish from her toe nails and replaced it with a new shimmery pink colour. As they dried, she sat with her legs in Jeremy's lap, pieces of cotton wool between her toes.

Even in the comfortable normalcy of their Sunday morning rituals, Susan was never far from the edges of their thoughts, a fact reflected in the abnormal lack of conversation between them.

Finally, just before ten o'clock, Rachel sat up. As she plucked the cotton wool balls from her toes, she announced, "I'm going to pick up a newspaper from the Shell station. Do you need anything?"

"We used the last of the grapes just now. See if they have any."

"Okey dokey. Be back in a few," Rachel said as she grabbed her keys, carefully pushed her feet in a pair of simple blue slippers that absolutely clashed with her green shirt and grey yoga pants ensemble, and headed outside. Jeremy heard the engine of the new Land Rover roar into life as she drove off.

Jeremy noted the time and switched channels to the local television channel, CBC TV, to watch the start of the third day of the cricket test between West Indies and Australia. Commentary was just beginning and Jeremy settled down to enjoy a little of the game.

Half hour later he heard the Defender pull into the driveway followed by the sound of the car door opening. Another five minutes elapsed and Rachel hadn't yet come inside.

Jeremy got up and looked through the living room window. The Defender was parked in the driveway with the driver's door open.

He stepped outside and scanned the area quickly before walking towards the vehicle.

On the ground outside the SUV, he found a newspaper, a plastic bag of groceries and a set of keys on a metallic key fob. He recognised the keys as Rachel's - for the car and the house. He picked up everything and under the bag was one blue slipper.

He looked around but there was no sign of his wife or anyone else.

With Susan's disappearance still fresh in his mind, he feared the worst.

"Rachel!" he yelled as he walked briskly around the side of the house. There was no response.

He stepped to the edge of the property and looked up and down the street. There was no one around and no traffic - just a typically quiet

Sunday morning in Rowan's Park.

Jeremy hurried back inside, closing the Defender's door on the way. He picked up the landline receiver just as his cell phone started to ring. He grabbed it and saw Rachel's name on the caller ID display.

"Rachel?"

A young male voice replied using raw Bajan dialect.

"Don' fuckin' call nuh police or we gine kill she fuh yuh. Wait fuh we to call you." The call ended with a smashing sound followed by sharp static.

Jeremy felt like his heart was trying to escape the confines of his chest. He immediately felt faint, forcing him to sit down at the dining room table, his entire body trembling uncontrollably. He dropped his cell phone on the table and just stared at it.

The television was still airing cricket from Antigua and the sound of the game filled the room. Jeremy was oblivious.

When he was able to, Jeremy picked up the cell phone and slowly dialled a number. After three rings Tiberius answered with slightly less joviality than usual.

"What's up JP? Anything new on the waitress?"

"Ti…" Jeremy began but couldn't get the words out.

Tiberius' voice became more serious. "Jeremy, what's the matter?"

"It's Rachel. She's…," Jeremy still couldn't complete the sentence.

"Is she ok?"

"She's… I don't know where she is." The last word was almost a whimper.

"I'm coming over, Jeremy. Give me twenty minutes."

"Tiberius."

"Yeah, I'm still here."

"Come armed."

Half hour later Tiberius was sitting at the dining room table with

Jeremy, who was sipping from a glass of water. He had spent the last several minutes listening as Jeremy brought him up to date on the situation.

"So you think she was grabbed just as she returned here. Did you hear anything strange at all? Like another vehicle?"

"I didn't hear anything out of the ordinary at all." Jeremy glanced towards the television. "I was engrossed in the game," he added quietly.

Tiberius stood and walked over to the window. "Do you think it was Shorey?"

"Who else would it be, Tiberius?" Jeremy snapped.

Tiberius returned to the table. "Look JP, don't you think we should still call the police?"

"No!" Jeremy said firmly as he launched himself from the table. He paced around the room with his hands on his head.

"They said they would kill her, Tiberius." He stopped pacing and looked at his friend. "I don't know what to do."

Tiberius walked over to the window once more and looked outside. "Do you think we're being watched?"

Jeremy turned to his friend for a few moments before heading to another window and scanned the exterior. Tiberius did the same at the kitchen window. The two continued this process until they had covered every window in the house. They met back in the living room a few minutes later.

"No sign of anyone or anything out of the ordinary," Tiberius revealed.

"I didn't see anything either," Jeremy agreed.

They both went to the sitting room and sat in front of the now muted television. Tiberius continued.

"How would they know if you called the police? Could they be scanning your cell phone?"

"This isn't a movie, Tiberius," Jeremy scoffed before adding, "But I guess it's possible."

"Of course it is. People use radio-wave scanners to monitor cell phone calls all the time," Tiberius suggested.

"What's more likely is that Shorey's friends in the force will alert him if I call." Jeremy said and then sighed loudly.

"But Ti, I can't just sit here and wait for them to call me. Rachel's life is in danger." He bowed his head, reluctant tears filling his eyes. "If she's still…" was all he could manage.

Tiberius moved from his seat to sit next to his friend. He placed a hand on his shoulder and said nothing for a few minutes.

"There must be someone on the force we can trust," Tiberius eventually said gently.

Jeremy wiped his eyes in one motion. "We met a detective on Friday night. He seemed like a straight shooter. But I don't remember…"

Jeremy paused for a moment before suddenly bolting from his seat and heading to the bedroom. He returned quickly, peering inside a wallet he was now holding. He produced a business card as he sat down.

"Detective Harold Mason," he read from the card.

"What do you want to do?"

Jeremy stared at the card, turning it over between his thumb and forefinger before responding. "We need to do something."

He picked up his cell phone but hesitated before dialling. He looked at Tiberius for a beat and then leaned across to pick up his cordless phone instead. He began dialling but stopped before completion.

"Cell phone. Cordless phone. It's all the same if we're being monitored?"

"Don't you have a wired back-up phone?" Tiberius queried.

Jeremy looked thoughtful for a moment before exclaiming, "We actually do!"

He got up and once more headed to the bedroom. He rummaged in the bottom of the wardrobe for a while before finding a plain, brown, cardboard box, covered in dust but otherwise unblemished.

Jeremy opened the box and took out a slim white telephone with a thick coiled wire connecting the receiver with the base.

He took it back to the living room and, as Tiberius watched, unplugged the cordless phone base to replace it with the wired version. He picked up the receiver and was relieved to hear a dial tone.

"Here we go," Jeremy said before dialling. He almost hung up after four rings but then the call was answered before the fifth.

"Mason, good morning."

"Detective Mason. This is, um, Jeremy Phillips."

There was a pause. "Mr. Phillips, what can I do for you?"

"There's been a development, but I'd rather not discuss it on the phone."

"I'm at home now, but do you want to meet me at the station?"

Jeremy hesitated. "I don't think that's a good idea. Do you mind if we meet somewhere else?" He looked at Tiberius, who was now pointing to his own chest.

"Let's meet at my friend's house in Prior Park." Jeremy gave some directions.

"I can be there in half hour," the detective said.

"Detective, can I ask you to come alone and not discuss this call with anyone?"

There was silence on the line for a few seconds before Mason responded. "That is contrary to RBPF regulations, Mr. Phillips," he said referring to the Royal Barbados Police Force.

"Sir, I have to ask you to do this. My wife's life may be in danger."

There was another pause. "Okay. I'll see you just before midday."

Mason ended the call and Jeremy hung up. He looked at Tiberius and exhaled before speaking.

"If it's really Shorey that took Rachel, I don't have any confidence that the police will be helpful. He's been a drug lord for years but has never been touched and it's because he has his own cronies in the force. So just involving the police may be dangerous for Rachel." Jeremy rubbed his eyes with his thumb and middle finger and bowed his head.

Tiberius was silent for a moment before speaking quietly. "JP, if that's what you think, why did you call this detective?"

Jeremy didn't immediately respond, but stood and wandered aimlessly towards the sitting room. He placed his hands on his head, fingers laced over the top.

"There is something about Mason that makes me think we can trust him. He seems like a straight laced, by the book type. A good guy. And he was so intense when he questioned us, he was definitely not just going through the motions. He wants to catch Shorey. Maybe he has for a long time. And he may not even know who he can trust within the police force."

Tiberius turned his head on the side like a dog listening to something. "You got all of this from one meeting, did you."

Jeremy walked over to the table and stood next to where Tiberius was sitting.

"The police may not be able to help me but maybe I can help myself, with Detective Mason's assistance."

"Jeremy, we don't know what happened to Rachel. Or Susan for that matter. How can you be making plans? And also, if Mason is such a straight shooter, why would he do anything other than whatever police do?"

"Because, Ti, helping me would help him. Let's get going to Prior Park. We can talk on the way."

"Mr. Phillips, abductions of any kind are serious criminal matters that require the full weight of the force to investigate and resolve," Mason said tersely.

The detective was sitting at Tiberius' dinner table across from Jeremy, while Tiberius leaned on the wall behind his friend. The relative positions bizarrely mirrored Jeremy and Rachel's interrogation at the police station less than thirty-six hours before.

"Detective, I am sure you're right, but I have every reason to believe that involving the police will put my wife's life in danger."

Mason held his hands out in front of him, palms up. "But you *have* involved the police."

Tiberius pulled up a chair and sat next to Jeremy.

"Sir, we know we're putting you in a bit of a situation by sharing this information and asking you not to act on it. But what would you do in our position?" Tiberius implored.

Mason answered quickly. "I would let the force handle the matter.

This is not a game."

Jeremy leaned forward and spoke quietly.

"Detective Mason, we know that Barrington Shorey is a major drug dealer. We've known for two years. When Rachel and I spoke to you on Friday, we didn't lie about not associating with him. We never have. But we do know what he's all about."

It was now Mason's turn to lean forward. "What exactly do you think you know?"

"I can give you some insight into his distribution network. It's second hand information but it's information nevertheless. All I'm asking for in return is your own insight into my situation and some information about Shorey."

Mason leaned back and folded his arms across his chest.

"You realise that you have just admitted to having knowledge of criminal activities. I can look at that in two ways. On the one hand, you may have a useful tip that could assist the force in apprehending an alleged criminal. I'd welcome such a tip and we can immediately adjourn this meeting and reconvene at the station so you can give your official statement."

Mason then placed his palms flat on the table and leaned forward, a hint of steel in his voice.

"On the other hand, based on your admitted knowledge of criminal activities, along with your personal relationships with two people who are now apparently missing, I have every reason to suspect that you, Mr. Phillips, are complicit in said criminal activities. I can simply have you arrested."

Jeremy swallowed audibly and could say nothing for a moment. Tiberius cleared his throat before speaking softly.

"Detective Mason, please hear us out. If you don't like what we have to say, you'll still have the option of taking us to the station for a statement or arresting us."

Mason looked at Tiberius and then Jeremy, before once more leaning back with his arms crossed in front of him. "Very well. But let me be frank. I have no intention of divulging anything that, in my judgement, jeopardises the integrity of any ongoing investigation."

Jeremy was nodding. "I wouldn't expect anything else."

"And if I don't like what I hear, I will leave and expect that you will find yourself at the Oistins Police Station immediately to make a full statement. Is that understood?"

Jeremy paused before responding. "Okay, I'll agree to that. And let me assure you that nothing we discuss here today will leave this room. You have our word."

Mason stared intensely at Jeremy before responding.

"Okay. Let's hear it."

Jeremy took a deep breath and began speaking.

"Detective, I have information that Shorey has friends in the force. I think this might be part of the reason that he has never been caught. If Shorey is really responsible for Rachel's disappearance, and we involve the police officially, he'll probably know immediately."

Mason didn't seem surprised by this information, so Jeremy continued

"The guy who called me earlier said that I would be contacted, with instructions I guess. Our suggestion is to wait for that call and see what they're asking for. Then we can act on it to suit. But what I need is as much information about Shorey as I can get, so I would have a bit of an advantage going forward."

Jeremy closed his eyes for a moment before continuing. "I plan on getting my wife back. And to do that, we may have to hurt some people. Do you understand what I'm saying?"

Mason sat motionless, looking at Jeremy for a while before commenting. "I believe I understand, but this seems like a fool's errand. What makes you think you'd have any hope of success against seasoned criminals?"

Tiberius chimed in. "They won't be expecting any real opposition if the police aren't involved so we'll have the element of surprise. And we do know our way around firearms if necessary. Legal firearms," he added quickly.

Jeremy continued. "Plus, what choice do we have? Going to the police is probably a death sentence for my wife. Doing nothing may be the same. Being proactive seems like my best option. And if I succeed, great. If I don't, you'll have a new angle to continue your investigations into Shorey."

Mason looked sceptical. "Not succeeding could mean your lives."

Jeremy squirmed briefly in his seat. "That's possible, but as Tiberius said, we know what we're doing and they're not expecting this."

"We're completely aware of the risks," Tiberius added.

Mason stood up and walked to a window. After staring outside for close to a minute he turned and looked at Jeremy.

"What do you want to know?"

Tiberius got up and returned with a yellow legal pad and a pen.

Jeremy started to ask questions.

Mason, after a reluctant beginning, started to answer.

They had been speaking for over an hour when Jeremy's cell phone rang. He looked down at it, glanced at Mason and turned the device so that the detective could see the 'unknown number' display. Mason made the '*go ahead*' signal by twirling his hand and Jeremy answered the call.

"Hello."

"Hello JP."

Jeremy felt like his blood had turned to ice. He hesitated before responding to a voice he had only heard a few times before.

"Mr. Shorey."

Shorey's voice was pleasant and cordial. "Oh you can call me Barry, JP."

Jeremy ground his teeth quietly. "What's up, Barry?"

"Well, it seems that something has happened to Susan." He then made a clicking noise with his tongue. "Oh what am I saying? You know this already. According to the news reports you actually discovered that she was missing, didn't you."

"Rachel and I did," Jeremy said mildly.

"Ah yes. How is your wife anyway?"

"I'm not sure," Jeremy said through gritted teeth.

"I assure you that's she's not doing well," Shorey said and paused for a beat. "After all, Rachel and Susan are very close so I imagine she's… broken up about all of this," Shorey said with a sincere congeniality that belied the apparent implication of his words.

Jeremy didn't respond. Shorey continued.

"To tell you the truth JP, I'm quite upset about the whole thing myself. And to make matters worse, I spent much of yesterday being questioned by police who seemed to know quite a bit about my business, especially as it relates to Susan. Can you believe that? Thankfully I have a solid alibi even though I don't know why I would need one."

"Mr. Shorey…"

"Come on JP, call me Barry. We're friends after all. And right now I could use a friend. Why not meet me so we can help each other get through this trying ordeal."

Jeremy swallowed and had difficulty saying anything for a few seconds. Then he cleared his throat and began to ask the only question that mattered.

"Barry, is Rachel okay?"

Shorey didn't hesitate. "I'm sure she'll be fine JP. She'll get through this. She's a strong girl after all. But let's chat about this in person.

Meet me at Esso Black Rock at two o'clock."

"You mean this afternoon?"

"I mean right now, JP," Shorey said firmly. "And even though Esso is a public place, we'll be having a private and personal conversation. So please, come alone. I can't emphasise how important that last point is."

Jeremy looked from Tiberius to Mason before responding. "Okay, I'll meet you there."

"Fantastic," Shorey exclaimed. "I'll see at two. Don't be late," he said before ending the call.

Jeremy held the phone to his ear for a few moments before slowly placing it on the table with trembling hands. He looked up to see Mason and Tiberius looking at him expectantly. He took a deep breath and then relayed the details of his conversation with Shorey.

Tiberius was the first to speak. "You're actually going to meet him?"

Jeremy stood up. "Yes, I am." He continued as he saw the disapproving look on Tiberius' face.

"Look, when they took Rachel, they could have easily come after me at the same time, so I'm guessing they don't want me like that. Plus, we'll be in a public place. I don't think I'm in danger."

Now Mason stood. "As we just discussed, Shorey may have friends in the force and has been very clever in his operations. But the main reason he has been able to maintain his cover as a legitimate businessman and elude the law, is by doing things quietly. His rivals have tended to simply disappear with no obvious signs of violence. I would suggest that meeting in a public place is a safe option for you."

Mason walked around the table to stand in front of Jeremy. "On the other hand, the abduction of your wife and the scene at Miss Farrell's home seem a little splashy for him. There may be other unpredictable factors at play here."

"Are you suggesting I don't go?"

Mason looked directly at Jeremy for a few seconds before responding.

"Mr. Phillips, you have asked me to treat this meeting as being outside of my law enforcement responsibilities. Because of that, I will say that the decision to go or not is entirely up to you. Were I wearing my official hat, however, I would say you should go straight to the station and report your wife's disappearance and that phone call."

Jeremy nodded. "Okay I'm…"

Mason cut him off. "I think it's best that I don't know your decision right now. However, whatever you decide, good luck Mr. Phillips."

Tiberius and Jeremy walked the detective outside. They were completely ignored by Tiberius' two Akitas who were lying in the driveway.

Mason shook hands with both men and drove off.

Tiberius turned to Jeremy.

"I'm guessing I can't talk you out of going."

"I'm going Ti."

"You do remember I have some first-hand knowledge of Shorey's kind. You know they don't mess around.

"I know."

Tiberius fished his keys from his pocket and handed them to Jeremy. "Well, take my car. And I left some security in the centre compartment. Just in case you need it."

Jeremy took the keys and shook his friend's hand. "Thanks Curt. I'll let you know how it goes."

He got in the car and drove off, thinking that he couldn't remember the last time he had called Tiberius by his real name.

It was thirteen minutes past two and Jeremy had been waiting at the Esso service station for twenty minutes.

He was watching every vehicle that entered the station through his rear view mirror, looking for Shorey's Range Rover. Eventually a nondescript grey Toyota Corolla with a dark window tint caught his attention. It was now driving slowly towards his parking space.

As Jeremy followed the progress of the car, he gently placed his hand on the centre console next to him.

The Corolla came to a stop next to Tiberius' Mazda. The near window slowly descended revealing Barrington Shorey in the passenger seat. The driver was obscured from his line of vision.

"Hello JP. Would you like to join me for a walk?"

Jeremy kept his eyes on Shorey, but his left hand tightened on the centre console which somehow began to feel hot to his touch. Then he relaxed his grip as he responded.

"Sure Barry."

They each got out of their cars and were soon joined by the Corolla's driver. Jeremy immediately recognised him as Adrian, Susan's young boyfriend. The stoic, scowling expression on his face was similar to the one he wore in the photograph Susan showed him and Rachel two years earlier.

Shorey was tall and fair-skinned with angular good looks. He was in his mid-forties and looked as if he knew his way around a gym. His simple, but expensive-looking black polo shirt was tucked into blue jeans, under which black running shoes were visible. He was carrying a broad brimmed straw hat, which he now casually placed on his shaved head.

He started walking towards the exit of the station, beckoning for Jeremy to join him. Jeremy fell into line with him while Adrian followed about a dozen paces behind.

Even on Sunday, there was regular vehicular and pedestrian traffic as they crossed the street and walked onto University Drive, the site of the University of the West Indies Cave Hill Campus. The street sloped gently at the start, becoming steeper the further you went. The university was at the midpoint of the hill.

"I usually go for a walk on Sunday mornings, but today there were a few distractions. So this is today's exercise for me. My apologies because I know you've already jogged today," Shorey said brightly.

Jeremy immediately had a sickening feeling in the pit of his stomach at the realisation that he and had wife had obviously been monitored early that morning. He slowed and then stopped walking.

"Mr. Shorey can you just tell me what you want from me."

Shorey looked back and then reversed his direction until he was standing in front of Jeremy. Jeremy glanced back to see that Adrian was standing stationary about ten feet behind him.

"It's Barry, remember. And I suppose here is as good a place as any," Shorey said as a mini-bus passed by, horn blaring loudly to make sure it was seen.

"JP, I need you to tell me what you did with the bag after you killed

Susan."

At first Jeremy wasn't sure he understood what Shorey was asking so he just looked at him. Shorey stared intently back at him.

"What? What do you…" Jeremy stammered finally.

Shorey spoke as if he was dealing with a child. "Come on JP, Susan told me only last week that you and your wife seemed a little too interested in my property. She said she overheard you all discussing some type of heist and she was actually fearful for her life."

Jeremy couldn't believe what he was hearing. "That's not true."

"To be honest I didn't believe it myself. You see I had already had you well vetted. Neither you nor your wife have a criminal record and you live perfectly vanilla lives. Although you are both on the kinky side I suppose. I guess in the end I underestimated you."

"Mr. Shorey, Barry, I don't know why Susan would have said that. We have never had any interest in your business."

"That's what I thought too. In fact when I suggested to Susan that she recruit you two years ago, I wasn't completely surprised that you didn't accept. But I did wonder why the two of you continued associating with her and never went to the authorities. Now I know. You were playing a game all along."

"I don't know what you're talking about. We don't know anything about your bag, and we didn't hurt Susan!" Jeremy raised his voice in desperation.

"I understand that your wife has been saying the same thing to my associates as well, even though our interrogation techniques have been quite robust. Which reminds me, she sent you something. Adrian!"

Adrian put his hand in his pocket as he walked towards them. He pulled it out and revealed a white plastic bag folded into a small square, which he now held towards Jeremy.

Jeremy looked at blankly, a feeling of dread washing over him.

"Take it JP, It's a gift from your wife," Shorey encouraged. "But you can open it later."

Jeremy took the plastic bag. There was hardly any weight to it.

When Shorey spoke again, some of the cordiality had left his voice. "I don't know how much more interrogation Rachel can take, so if I were you, I'd be looking to return my property as soon as possible."

He looked at his watch. "You have until forty-eight hours from right now before the interrogation ends. It will end suddenly, if you get my meaning. The only reason I'm giving you so much time is that my associates find your wife very attractive and have been enjoying certain aspects of the interrogation process. I'm giving them time to indulge."

Jeremy felt a sharp anger growing inside but said nothing.

Shorey stepped even closer to Jeremy and whispered. "Just to be clear, if you don't return my property by two thirty on Tuesday, you'll never see your wife alive again. And you won't live too much longer after that."

He stepped past Jeremy and walked in the direction of the Esso station, shouting over his shoulder as he walked.

"I'll call you at two thirty on Tuesday, JP. I imagine you'll have good news for me. Otherwise I'll have bad news for you."

Adrian stayed in position, staring at Jeremy with an inscrutable expression for a few moments, before turning and following his boss downhill.

Jeremy watched them leave until he remembered the folded plastic bag he was holding.

He opened it slowly and looked inside. He immediately felt sick.

Inside was a human toe with a shimmery pink nail polish that he recognised.

Chapter 11

West Indies vs Sri Lanka
Galle, Sri Lanka

Day 5 Report
Muttiah Muralitharan spun Sri Lanka to their first Test
victory against the West Indies as the tourists' batting
betrayed their lack of experience and confidence against
top class spin.

West Indies had realistic hopes of victory for much of this
test, but now leave Galle one-down and distraught.

Saturday, November 17th, 2001

"Do you realise this will be three days in a row we're seeing Susan? It's like we're dating her now."

Jeremy and Rachel were driving towards Kingsland Terrace at Susan's invitation. It was just after five in the evening after a relaxing Saturday recovering from Friday night's exertions.

Jeremy was behind the wheel of his Mitsubishi and Rachel was giggling at his comment.

"You seemed quite happy last night. And the night before."

Jeremy was forced to smile from the memories. "It wasn't a complaint, just an observation," he admitted.

"I see. Observation noted," Rachel stated cheerfully. "Anyway, as I told you, she's inviting us over for a drink to discuss something. A business proposal apparently."

Jeremy glanced at his wife sharply before returning his attention to the road. "You didn't mention the business proposal part before. Did she give you any idea of what type of business?"

"She didn't."

"Oh Lord. I bet you it's AMWAY," Jeremy groaned.

Rachel laughed. "It's not AMWAY, JP"

"Are you sure? Rachel is exactly their target market: underemployed. And this is their M.O." Jeremy then mimicked a confident female voice. "'*I have a business proposition to discuss with you*' and then *wham…* you're sitting at an AMWAY cult meeting."

Rachel continued to laugh. "Your imagination is too wild."

"Don't blame my imagination, I have first-hand knowledge. Let's just say that I've been fooled before. The last time was by my former lawyer. I really thought he had a genuine business proposal."

"You mean it's happened more than once? Are you sure that doesn't automatically make you a member?" Rachel asked cheekily.

Jeremy sucked his teeth, prompting new peals of laughter from his wife.

They turned into Susan's driveway and parked behind her CRV.

"No other vehicles around," Jeremy observed. "That rules out a cult meeting ambush. So it'll be a solo pitch to draw us in, then."

"Oh hush,' Rachel admonished as she exited the car. They headed to the front door, holding hands, smiles all around. Susan opened the door moments after they knocked.

"Look who's here, my favourite people in the world," Susan exclaimed as she greeted them each with a hug and a kiss on the cheek.

"Come in. I have so much to discuss with you." She turned and led them into the living room.

Jeremy turned to Rachel and mouthed a silent 'AMWAY'. Rachel elbowed him playfully in the ribs and walked ahead.

They settled on the comfortable living room furniture while Susan busied herself with opening a bottle of red wine.

They chatted casually for a while on topics ranging from the tribulations of Susan's relationships with Barry and Adrian; interesting work stories from Rachel especially; the war in Iraq and even sports. Susan was into cricket so she and Jeremy spoke a bit about the game the West Indies lost against Sri Lanka earlier that day.

Not being a huge fan, Rachel was quiet during the cricket conversation. When they began to argue about whether or not the West Indies could win any of the games in Sri Lanka, Rachel interrupted.

"As fascinating as this is, Susan, we really want to hear about this business proposal of yours."

Susan looked at Rachel and then took a sip of her wine. "You're so impatient, Rachel." She sighed dramatically. "Anyway I guess it would be easier to show you. Follow me."

Susan placed her glass on the coffee table and headed towards the bedrooms. Rachel and Jeremy did the same.

When Susan reached the guest bedroom she produced a key ring with two keys from her pants pocket, unlocked and opened the door and stepped inside.

Jeremy and Rachel followed her into a room that they had only glimpsed previously, and watched as Susan dragged one of the many boxes on the floor over to the dresser. She stood on it so she could reach the storage area above. When it was opened, they could see a large, black bag inside, which Susan struggled to remove. Jeremy walked over and helped her take the bag down, surprised at how heavy it was.

Once it was on the floor, Susan dropped onto her haunches next to it. They could now see that it was a large Adidas duffel bag, almost three feet long by eighteen inches wide and high. Next to the bag, Susan's frame seemed especially petite, as she crouched there, smiling, before unzipping it.

From Jeremy's vantage point, the first thing he saw inside was metallic surfaces that he couldn't identify. When Susan pulled the opening wider apart, he recognised a number packets, each roughly the size and shape of a deck of cards and wrapped in aluminium foil. He started to suspect what they were and hoped he was wrong.

He tore his attention away from the bag and back to Susan, who was still smiling at them. He heard his wife begin to speak.

"Susan, what is all of this?"

"This, dearies, is what one point five million dollars in heroin looks like. I'm talking US dollars."

The couple said nothing, but alternated incredulous gazes from the Susan to the bag and back.

"Well, say something, guys," Susan implored.

"Susan, what have you gotten yourself into?" Rachel asked quietly.

Susan stood. "I have gotten myself into money, bitches."

Jeremy suddenly snapped his fingers, and blurted "Barrington Shorey. I remember how I know the name."

Rachel glanced at him. "What? What does that…"

Jeremy interrupted her. "It was a few years ago but it was a big story for a short time." He turned to Rachel. "A container of drugs was seized by police and apparently it was addressed to a local company. The owner of the company was initially suspected and questioned, before an employee confessed that he was responsible."

Rachel was just staring at him while Susan smiled knowingly.

"The company was Absolute Shore-ity. Barrington Shorey's company," he finally announced.

Susan was nodding. "Barry is more than just a successful business owner, he is also a bit of a facilitator. I'll explain after I put this back."

Jeremy helped her return the bag to the storage area and they headed to the living room, with Susan locking the door behind them.

Once the three were seated, wine glasses in hand, Susan began speaking.

"There are people that need to get certain products from South America to Europe and Barbados is one of the transhipment points." Susan took a sip, looking at the couple as if she was ensuring they understood exactly what she was talking about.

She continued as if she was reading a script

"Barry facilitates this by storing the products in Barbados until the second leg of the shipment can start. Sometimes he uses other people for storage and he pays them well. He's very selective about who he chooses - no criminals or high profiles. That's where people like me and you come in."

"Susan..." Rachel began.

"It isn't even always that type of stuff," Rachel interrupted, pointing to the guest bedroom. "Sometimes it's only cash. Large quantities of cash, mind you. But I think this could be a great opportunity for you guys."

The couple was quiet for a while and then Jeremy spoke up.

"Susan, are you asking us to participate in international drug dealing?"

Susan laughed. "Not at all. I see it as offering storage services to a transnational corporation."

Jeremy looked at Rachel, who was staring blankly at Susan, and then responded.

"We appreciate this offer, Susan, but we think we'll stay away from a life of crime. Rachel wouldn't do well in prison," Jeremy added, trying to lighten the mood slightly.

"You need to worry about your own ass in prison. Literally." Rachel retorted.

Susan put down her glass and shifted to the edge of the seat, leaning towards the couple.

"But that's just it. There's no real risk. Barry has friends in the police, even in the drug squad. He's always forewarned on the rare occasions that police are getting too close."

"If that's the case, how did he almost get caught with that shipment a few years ago?" Jeremy asked.

"That was actually a set up. Another distributor was trying to put Barry out of business by planting a shipment and tipping off the police."

"Well, couldn't that happen again?" Jeremy asked.

Susan picked up her drink and sipped, before responding evenly. "No. That distributor definitely won't be doing that again."

Rachel spoke up. "But hold on. Jeremy, didn't you say that an employee confessed?"

Jeremy nodded as Susan explained. "That's just one example of how loyal Barry's people are. That guy was willing to go to jail to protect Barry. Isn't that something?"

Jeremy looked at Susan, wondering whether she was being clever or naive.

"It's something all right," was all he said.

"Susan, all of this talk about product and distributor and facilitator is bullshit. You're just talking about dealing drugs," Rachel said with an edge to her voice.

Susan seemed especially relaxed as she responded. "When did you become such a stick in the mud, Rachel? All I'm doing is offering storage for a shipment that will not end up in Barbados. Will not affect Bajans at all. And I'm making decent money. You should at least consider it."

Rachel gave Susan a withering look but said nothing.

"Susan, no offence, but I don't think this is for us," Jeremy volunteered.

"But we do appreciate you thinking of us and offering the opportunity, right Rachel?"

The scowl momentarily remained on Rachel's face but then she sighed and her expression softened. "Okay Susan. I guess your heart was in the right place."

"Aww sweetie," Susan squealed as she got up and dropped into Rachel's lap. "Are you sure you won't reconsider? It's easy money."

"No, Susan. As JP said, this isn't for us. But if you're comfortable and happy with it, good for you." She caressed Susan's cheek. "And there will be no judgement from us, right Jeremy?"

"No," said Jeremy mildly.

"Fine then. Your loss," Susan said as she got to her feet and reached into her pocket. "But I do have a gift for you." She produced the set of keys.

"I have to travel from time to time for Barry. Sometimes it's just overnight but it can be as long as a week. I just need you to water my plants and clear my mail, so these are your keys to my place. Is that okay?"

"Absolutely," Rachel responded and took the keys.

"Why do you have to travel so often?" Jeremy asked.

"It's usually just to pick up important documents and stuff," Susan said vaguely.

"Okay," Jeremy said, unconvinced.

"Anyway, now you have keys to my place, you can pop by anytime," Susan said. She looked at Rachel.

"I hope I haven't spoiled what we have." She glanced at Jeremy. "What we all have."

Rachel hugged Susan and motioned for Jeremy to join them. After the briefest of pauses, he got up and wrapped his arms around both of them.

"We're good, Susan," Rachel said.

They continued chatting and finished the bottle of wine, after which Rachel and Jeremy left.

There was no conversation for first few minutes and then Rachel broke the silence.

"At least it wasn't AMWAY."

"Not funny Rachel," Jeremy replied tersely. "This is a very bad idea. We should not be associating with that girl. We could easily find ourselves in big trouble. I don't care how many friends Shorey has in the force."

Rachel looked contemplative for a few moments before responding.

"We aren't in her business, JP. We're just her friends. There's no law against that."

"But Rachel…" Jeremy began.

"We just need to continue doing what we're doing, having fun, no more than that. Nothing to do with Shorey and his drug dealing self. Plus, Susan would never let anything bad happen to us. It'll be fine."

"You realise that just the appearance of associating with criminals could be disastrous for our careers, right? Guilty by association and all of that."

"You're suggesting I get rid of a friend just because she likes bad boys?"

Jeremy's tone was measured. "Rachel, we're talking about drug dealers here, serious gangsters. On an international scale apparently." He then remembered something from earlier. "By the way, did you hear what she said about the Absolute Shore-ity employee taking the fall for his boss? Do you think that happened out of loyalty? Bullshit!"

Rachel was staring straight ahead without responding.

Jeremy continued, his tone betraying more emotion with each sentence.

"It's possible that '*loyalty*' was gained by Shorey guaranteeing the employee's family would be well taken care when he went to prison. But I'm betting that it was more the promise that the employee *AND* his family would suffer horrible deaths if he didn't take responsibility for the drug shipment. Rachel, that's how these drug guys operate. They do not play!"

"You seem to know a lot about drug guys."

Jeremy allowed his smouldering anger to subside before he responded.

"I know a bit. Thanks to Tiberius."

Rachel looked at her husband quizzically but said nothing. Jeremy inhaled deeply and released the breath slowly before speaking.

"Ti's family was originally from St. Vincent. They moved here when he and his younger brother Andrew were very young. Andrew moved back to St. Vincent when he was fifteen and got involved in some illegal shit. Ended up running back to Barbados to get away, owing the wrong people a lot of money."

Jeremy hesitated before continuing. Rachel did not interrupt the silence.

"Months later, those guys followed him here. Andrew disappeared one day only to be discovered days later in a cane field with a bullet in his head and each hand chopped off. He was twenty years old."

Rachel looked shocked. "I remember that incident. It was about ten years ago, right? I didn't know it was Ti's brother."

Jeremy nodded. "I got the full story from Ti, including the threats made against him and his family. That incident is the real reason Tiberius and I started learning to shoot."

"I see."

"Drug guys do not play," Jeremy reiterated under his breath.

They drove in silence for a while longer.

"JP, I get what you're saying, but we will never get involved in this drug business. We will never associate with Barry. But Susan is a friend and I won't throw her to the wayside." Rachel turned to look through the passenger window before adding, "Like last time."

Jeremy paused before responding. "Well, she's your friend and you know best what she's all about. But I have a very bad feeling about all of this."

"I'll talk to Susan and let her know that we categorically want nothing to do with that part of her life," Rachel said just as Jeremy's cell phone started ringing.

He took his eyes off the road for a moment to glance at the caller ID before answering. "Good evening, Martin," he said with mild surprise in his voice.

"Hello Jeremy," his boss responded. "Sorry to call you on a weekend but just wanted to update you on two things. Neither good I'm afraid."

Jeremy was concerned. "What's up?"

"Well, we didn't get the Olympio Lottery account unfortunately. The chairman filled me in at golf today. He did say that everyone was impressed by our presentation though, but they thought it would be better to go with a larger agency with greater resources than we have. Just thought I would let you know before you hear anything. You know how news travels in Bim," Chandler said, using one of the local nicknames for Barbados.

Jeremy was slightly crestfallen by the news. "Oh well. We gave it our best shot. We'll get 'em next time though."

"Yes we will," Chandler agreed confidently. "But the other news, do you remember Mrs Barrett?"

Jeremy drew a blank for a moment before remembering. "Oh you mean our Belleville neighbour?"

"Yes. Well, she passed away today."

"Oh no," Jeremy exclaimed gently.

"I remembered how instrumental you were in persuading us to repair her roof a few years ago. I figured you'd want to know."

"Yes. Thanks for telling me."

"No problem. You should also know that the company will pay for her funeral. She was our neighbour after all. I'd like you to represent the company at the funeral as well."

"Of course, Martin. That's very generous by the way."

"Credit yourself Jeremy. Your influence in handling her situation made us better corporate citizens. Much appreciated."

"Thanks," Jeremy said sheepishly.

"Well, enjoy the rest of weekend, Jeremy."

"You too, Martin."

They ended the call and he updated his wife with the details of the conversation.

"Sorry to hear, honey. I don't mean to sound insensitive but I'm more bummed about Olympio. I know you put a lot of effort into it."

"Yeah," Jeremy said simply, lost in his thoughts.

He was reviewing all the negativity he had absorbed in the last hour and felt a growing sense of dread.

He couldn't help but think that it was all a bad omen for the future.

Chapter 12

West Indies vs Australia
St. John's, Antigua

Day 4 Report
Australia looked set to wrap things up by tea before Sarwan and Chanderpaul brought West Indies back into contention.

At the close, Australia need four wickets to complete their victory, while West Indies need 47 runs for a historic achievement - the highest successful run chase in test cricket.

Monday, May 12th, 2003

By the time Jeremy woke up, he had come to a realisation: in order to save his wife's life, and his own, he had to kill Barrington Shorey.

He had spent a fitful night on Tiberius' sofa and now sat up and raised his arm to look at his watch. It was thirty-seven minutes past five in the morning.

As he lowered his arm, his focus shifted to the coffee table in front of him. And the folded plastic bag on it.

Jeremy leaned back and stared at the ceiling, thinking about everything that happened in the last few days: from Susan's disappearance, to Rachel's abduction and then his own encounter with Barrington Shorey.

After that meeting he had driven back to Tiberius' house, updated him and then spent the rest of the day and night quietly working through the problem in his mind:

- *Shorey was giving the impression that he had nothing to do with Susan's disappearance and the missing bag*
- *He blamed Rachel and himself*
- *This was due to lies Susan apparently told him a few days before she disappeared*
- *Shorey grabbed Rachel and threatened to kill her and him if the bag wasn't returned*
- *Jeremy didn't have the bag or knew where it could be*
- *Police couldn't be involved because of Shorey's connections*
- *He estimated that there was a better than fifty-fifty chance that Rachel was already dead*

Jeremy had ruminated over these details for hours before finally falling asleep from sheer mental exhaustion.

Awake now, and with this morning's realisation of what he had to do, he determined to figure out how to actually go about doing it.

"I just knew that woman was going to be bad news for us someday," he said aloud as he rose from the sofa and headed to the kitchen, suddenly aware that he was ravenous. It dawned on him that he hadn't eaten anything since breakfast with his wife the previous day.

"Did you say something?" Tiberius yelled from the bedroom.

"Talking to myself," Jeremy replied.

Tiberius lived in a two-story house neatly situated in the most westerly section of Prior Park, another upper middle class district similar to Rowans Park where Jeremy lived.

The house was originally built in the early 1970s when Prior Park wasn't much more than a few disparate homes dotted throughout several acres of undeveloped lots.

Due to the area's favourable proximity to the luxurious West coast and the fast developing Warrens area, land in Prior Park became very much in demand over the years.

The area expanded far beyond its original footprint. What was originally just called Prior Park became Prior Park Terrace and gave birth to Prior Park Gardens and Prior Park Crescent nearby.

Thanks to the emigrating previous owners, Tiberius bought the house at a relative steal eight years previously in 1995. With his brother's death still fresh in his mind, he immediately set out to make it into his own personal fortress.

He began renovating from day one, fortifying windows and doors with motorised metallic storm shutters and adding a ten foot tall brick and mortar perimeter wall with an electric gate. He installed the best monitored security system he could afford and as a final touch, bought and trained two Akita puppies who were now accomplished guard dogs.

He also started collecting what had become a small arsenal of firearms - mainly handguns, mostly legal.

This superior security relative to his own home was the reason Jeremy chose to overnight there, and also the reason he wasn't overly paranoid when he woke up.

Tiberius entered the kitchen wearing just shorts and glasses, but seemed very alert, as if he had been awake for a while. Jeremy was in the middle of preparing some omelettes.

"Wow. My houseguest making breakfast in the morning. You're better than most of the girls that sleep over. Except for the no sex part. Unless you're up for it, cause then you'd be the perfect guest."

Jeremy chuckled humourlessly but didn't immediately comment. But as he shovelled the first omelette into a plate, he blandly announced his intention to kill Shorey. Tiberius nodded once sharply and then opened the refrigerator to remove a carton of orange juice.

Both men had decided to take some vacation days to deal with Jeremy's situation. Soon they were sitting at the dining room table eating in silence, each seemingly lost in thought.

The yellow legal pad Tiberius had used the previous day to take notes during their session with Mason was still on the table. Towards the end of the meal, Jeremy pulled it closer and started scanning Tiberius' barely legible writing.

"Ti, I'm so glad you took these notes because I am drawing a blank when I try to remember much of what Mason told us yesterday."

"I'm no doctor, even though I've pretended to be one on many occasions. You know, to impress chicks. But even a periodic fake doctor like me can tell that you're still in shock from yesterday. Think of what you've been through, what you're still going through. The fact that you're not an absolute wreck right now is actually a symptom of that shock. It definitely explains the blanks in your memory," Tiberius offered.

"Thanks, fake doc," Jeremy said looking at the pad in hope that it would jog his memory. "I think, the first thing we have to determine is where he's holding Rachel. So we should review all of Shorey's properties, right?"

"Makes sense," Tiberius admitted with a shrug.

"So let's go through the list Mason gave us. If only I could understand your scribbles."

"Oh give it here," Tiberius said, holding out his hand. Jeremy gave him the legal pad and Tiberius started reading aloud.

"His main address is in Rendezvous. His mother lives in Rock Hall, St. Thomas in a house he owns. There's also a beach house in Cattlewash." The latter was a district on the East coast of the island consisting primarily of vacation homes.

Tiberius read to himself for a few moments before he continued.

"Then there are his businesses. Absolute Shore-ity Construction has two other show homes like Susan's. One is just around the corner in that new development in Clermont and the other is in St. Silas Heights. Both the construction and landscaping companies are in the Lower Estate commercial area."

"Yeah, I remember where the offices are. It's right next to the quarry," Jeremy said with a sigh.

"So let's start eliminating. Residential areas like Rendezvous and Rock Hall seem unlikely. She was taken in broad daylight so I don't see how they could smuggle her into a house in the middle of a busy neighbourhood without being seen. And heard for that matter, especially if…" Tiberius allowed his voice to trail off.

"Especially If they've been hurting her," Jeremy finished flatly. "The screams… they'd be noticed."

"Yes. Sorry," Tiberius said without looking at his friend. "Depending on where exactly in Cattlewash the beach house is located, that might be a possibility."

"Okay. What else? The construction company by the quarry seems like a good option."

"Hmmm. Maybe on the weekend but from today that place should be filled with workmen. What about the show homes?"

They looked at each other for a few moments, before Tiberius spoke.

"You know, we didn't ask Mason if the other show homes were inhabited."

"Shit! You're right," Jeremy exclaimed. "Okay, let's come back to that. Were there any other construction projects?"

Tiberius turned a few pages. "Mason mentioned the community centre in Haynesville. It's only recently finished and is apparently a passion project of Stetson Aimey, the lawyer, who is also an old school friend of Shorey. Mason lists him as part of the extended inner circle."

Tiberius looked up from the pad. "He's a lawyer though. He wouldn't be involved in any of this would he? Or am I being naive?"

"I don't know. But he's a long time friend so anything's possible. I mean, look what you're doing for me today."

"In my case it's because I'm a saint but I get your point," Tiberius said as he got up and went into the kitchen. He returned moments later with an open telephone directory.

"I think we can rule out Haynesville but let's see where Aimey lives," he said as he returned to the table. He found the name quickly.

"Hmmm, Heywoods Estate. Those houses are pretty spread out over there."

Jeremy contemplated this information briefly before commenting. "Add it to the list. Who else is in Shorey's inner circle"

Tiberius returned his attention to the pad and turned a page.

"Right. He said that Shorey has four main lieutenants - Patrick Blackman, Jabari Forde, Adrian Barrett and Ishmael Mansour. They are his bodyguards, enforcers, drivers and errand boys all twisted together. They've all had run-ins with the law at various times, so as they say, they are known to the police. Mason thinks that other than Aimey, they are the only people Shorey trusts and at least one is always near him."

"What about women? I remember Mason saying something."

Tiberius responded without referring to the notes. "Mason used the word '*lone wolf*' to describe Shorey's romantic life. He keeps women at arms length and actually seems to prefer working girls. Susan is the closest he has to a significant other, and as you know, even she had limited interaction with him."

Jeremy made a face and nodded slowly. "So the circle is small. But that still means that when I approach Shorey, I'll probably have to deal with up to four guys. Five if Aimey is involved."

"It's not like you'll be alone, JP. With me on your team we'll have an unfair advantage. I almost feel sorry for them."

Jeremy smiled, an action that would not be repeated that day.

Or the next day.

They had been going through the notes and thrashing out a plan for a while when Jeremy glanced at his watch and realised that it was approaching eight o'clock.

"Let's take a break. We both have some phone calls to make anyway."

Tiberius stood and stretched. "I'm going to feed the dogs. I don't know how much time I'll have for them today.

Jeremy used his mobile phone to make his first call to Warrens Motors and explained to Rachel's admin assistant that she was under the weather and wouldn't be in for a few days.

Then he called his office and spoke to Martin to formalise the request for three vacation days to deal with an unexpected family situation. Tiberius would be making a similar call to TravelWise.

Jeremy then grabbed the legal pad and stepped into the kitchen. He used Tiberius' landline there to make his final call to Detective Mason, who answered on the second ring.

"Mason."

"Good morning Detective."

"Mr. Phillips. How are you doing?" Mason asked with no discernible change in tone.

"I'm as well as can be expected."

"Any changes you need to apprise me of?"

Jeremy hesitated before responding. "Not really."

Mason inhaled as if he was about to speak but said nothing. Jeremy understood the pause as Mason wanting to ask about the meeting with Shorey but couldn't while wearing his figurative police hat.

"Detective, I have a quick question. The show homes that we spoke about yesterday, are they occupied?"

"Yes," he answered curtly.

"Do you know by whom?"

"Employees."

Jeremy recognised that Mason was uncomfortable with the conversation but he had one more query.

"One other thing: is there any way I can get access to photographs of persons who have been in trouble with the law?'

There was a brief pause before Mason answered. "Who exactly?"

Jeremy read from the legal pad.

"Patrick Blackman, Jabari Forde, Adrian Barrett and Ishmael Mansour. Actually forget Adrian, just the others."

The pause was longer this time. "Unfortunately it would be against regulations for me to provide that." He seemed to be choosing his words carefully. "Anyway, there's a lot happening in the island right now. Or don't you read the newspaper?"

It was now Jeremy's turn to pause. "I do. But I haven't read one today."

"I think you should. The Advocate is a good place to start. I think you would find it informative."

"All right," said Jeremy uncertainly.

"Good. Well, I hope you have a productive day. All the best."

Mason ended the call.

Tiberius returned from feeding the dogs and noticed Jeremy's studious expression. He made a wordless query by spreading his arms, palms up.

Jeremy looked at him, shrugged and said, "I think I need to buy a newspaper."

_____

Jeremy had borrowed Tiberius' car and hurried to a nearby roadside newspaper vendor, who seemed intent on engaging Jeremy in talk about the cricket in Antigua. Jeremy was uncharacteristically brusque in his response, paid for a newspaper and sped away.

Now back at the dining room table, Jeremy leafed through the issue of The Barbados Advocate, the older of the two main newspaper publishers on the island, but also the less popular. Under normal circumstances he would have read The Nation instead, and would certainly have missed the article he now found on page seventeen.

It was a society page depicting the opening of the community centre in Haynesville. The page was dominated by a series of candid photographs of officials and guests.

A few of the photos included Stetson Aimey interacting with other persons, usually smiling broadly. One of those pictures caught Jeremy's attention. It showed Aimey in conversation with a middle-aged lady while Shorey looked on. Jeremy glanced at the photo caption:

> L-R: Lawyer Stetson Aimey; Haynesville Community Group president, Dorothy Puckerin; Absolute Shore-ity Construction CEO, Barrington Shorey.

What really drew Jeremy attention, however, were three other men behind Shorey in the photograph. They were each wearing beige Absolute Shore-it polo shirts and were looking in three different directions with what looked like practised casualness. It reminded Jeremy of the security detail when a world leader is physically interacting with the public.

He pointed to that part of the photograph.

"I think this is what Mason wanted me to see. These guys here, acting like the blasted secret service. I bet they are three of Shorey's crew: Blackman, Forde and Mansour I'm guessing. This has to be Mason's way of helping me without helping me."

Tiberius, who was standing over Jeremy's shoulder, leaned to get a closer look. "I think you're right. Two black guys and a Syrian looking dude. It fits."

Jeremy continued scanning the other photographs. "I'm looking for Adrian, but I don't see him in any of these photos."

Tiberius stood upright. "JP, do you notice when this opening took place?"

Jeremy scanned through the page. "It was last Friday." He shifted in his chair to look at Tiberius. "Huh."

"'*Huh*' is right. That's the day Susan went missing. And look at the pictures. Some are in daylight and some are after dark. It was a pretty long event."

Jeremy saw where Tiberius was heading. "You're saying that this is a hell of an alibi for Shorey and his guys." He contemplated his own words for a moment before continuing.

"Yes, it conveniently does, but I'm already way past that. I don't believe he had anything to do with Susan's disappearance. As Mason said, it's not his style. Too showy."

"Agreed. Unless that's the point. Suppose the showiness is just to shift suspicion away from him. Maybe while Shorey was alibiing himself with canapés at a public event, the conspicuously absent Adrian guy was doing the dirty work in the splashiest way possible."

Jeremy pondered this. "Good points. But then why go to all the trouble of grabbing Rachel and threatening me if he already has his bag of stuff? For appearances?"

"Good question. We'll have to ask him when we see him."

"Yeah sure," Jeremy said as he removed the society page from the newspaper and stood up.

"You have some more calls to make and I have to take a shower before we hit the road. Do you have anything that would fit me?"

"Sure. I have a drawer full of T-shirts for my visiting lady friends. They'll fit you perfectly."

"A stakeout," Tiberius muttered. "I'm on a freaking stakeout. I cannot believe that Jeremy Garfield Phillips tricked me into being on a stakeout on the hottest freaking day of the year."

They were sitting in a silver Suzuki SUV, parked behind a small grove of trees in St. Silas Heights, St. James.

It was a cloudless, sunny day and at just after three o'clock the temperature in the car was approaching unbearable, even in the shade from the mature mahogany trees.

From their location, they could see the one hundred and fifty year old Anglican church that gave St. Silas Heights its name, but most of their range of vision was taken up by a breathtaking view of the West coast of the island and the ocean beyond.

However, their attention was on the Absolute Shore-ity Construction show home about six hundred feet downhill from their location. Jeremy was scrutinising the house though binoculars.

St. Silas Height was a relatively new development, created by subdividing former plantation land into lots. Only a few of them had been purchased so far so the show home was relatively isolated. That and the presence of a familiar looking Toyota Corolla parked in the driveway made them think that Rachel could be inside.

They had spent the day discreetly visiting the various locations on the shortlist they had compiled. Their theory was that wherever Rachel was being held, there would have to be some form of security, which meant someone from Shorey's inner circle or Shorey himself would have to be around at all times.

They had visited the show home in Clermont, the Absolute Shore-ity offices in Lower Estate, Shorey's beach house and Stetson Aimey's home, none of which showed any signs of the type of activity they were looking for.

Now, in St. Silas Heights, looking at the lonely show home and the car Jeremy recognised as the one Adrian and Shorey drove when he met with them the previous day, they thought they were in the right place.

"I can't take this heat," Tiberius said as he turned on the Suzuki's engine, rolled up the windows and dialled up the air conditioning. The compact SUV was compliments of the first stop on their road trip - the home of Tiberius' friend, Fiona - where they swapped vehicles. Fiona's Suzuki Vitara allowed them to carry out their undercover operations and its versatility was the reason they were able to park off-road on the current reconnaissance mission.

Jeremy welcomed the blast of cool air but still looked over to the show home to see if there was any reaction there to the sound of the car's engine. He saw none.

Since Jeremy left home that morning, he had slowly started to appreciate the seriousness of what they were planning, as well as how dangerous it was. He had become more apprehensive and agitated as the day progressed, and though he did his best not to show it, he realised that he was now on the verge of panic.

"Ti, can this plan even work? Can we really rescue Rachel from career criminals without getting ourselves killed and also get rid of a major gangster? This isn't a movie, man. I'm no Bruce Willis."

"Look who's finally coming out of his shock and reentering the real world," Tiberius said with his eyes closed, enjoying the air conditioning.

Jeremy looked at his friend. "You do think this can work, right?"

Tiberius opened his eyes but looked straight ahead. "I think we have a chance. They won't be expecting this move from us and we'll be armed to the teeth."

He turned to look at Jeremy. "Plus, what choice do we have?"

Jeremy was about to comment when a brief high-pitched sound floated towards their location. It sounded like a lady's voice but was cut off quickly.

The guys looked at each other and then over to the house.

The St. Silas show home was almost identical to the Kingsland Terrace version where Susan lived. The main difference was the landscaping, which was a lot less developed in the St. Silas house.

From their vantage point they could see little more than the eastern side of the house, where two large windows separated by a smaller one were visible. From Jeremy's memory of the layout of Susan's home, he worked out that the master bedroom and bathroom along with the living room were on that side. All three sets of curtains were drawn, preventing any visibility into the house from their position.

"Did that sound like a scream?" Jeremy asked.

"I'm not sure, but it was definitely a female," Tiberius said haltingly.

They were still staring at the house when a man dressed in a white vest and jeans came into view from the western side and headed to the Toyota. He was wiping his hands into a rag as he walked.

"That's Adrian," Jeremy confirmed and handed the binoculars to Tiberius.

He watched as Adrian put the rag into his back pocket, opened the passenger door and without sitting, rummaged in the glove compartment for a while.

Tiberius passed the binoculars back to Jeremy. "Look at the rag."

Jeremy adjusted the focus on the binoculars as Tiberius asked, "Does that look like blood?"

Jeremy zeroed in on the rag which did look blood-stained. Adrian soon apparently found what he was searching for, slammed the door shut and went back inside the house.

Jeremy lowered the binoculars. "This is the place."

"Looks that way," Tiberius agreed. "Let's get out of here. We have some work to do."

It was after ten o'clock that night and Jeremy was driving Rachel's Land Rover Defender because, as Tiberius said, '*it's built like a tank and can handle anything thrown at it*'.

Tiberius was in the backseat checking and rechecking the weapons he had chosen from his collection. There were two Glock 27 handguns - a model that Jeremy used regularly during his visits to the range at Kendal - and a brand new Beretta 92G-SD semi-automatic. Tiberius also carried a hunting knife in a sheath on his belt.

Both men were wearing caps, dark coloured long sleeved shirts, slacks and running shoes.

A few minutes earlier they had left Fiona's SUV at Jeremy's house and were now on Highway 2A on the way to St. Silas Heights.

The plan was to park downhill from the show home, sneak up to it on foot and execute a home invasion to rescue Rachel, using what Tiberius referred to as *lethal force* on anyone else present. Tiberius had emphasised repeatedly that the element of surprise would be the most effective weapon in their armoury.

Rachel was their priority, but they accepted that there was no guarantee that this part of their mission would be successful. If it turned out that Rachel was not actually being held where they thought or was already dead or if any other scenario of failure occurred, there was still a second phase to be executed, so to speak. As long as one or both of the guys survived, phase two was killing Shorey at his home in Rendezvous before he was aware of the St. Silas Heights operation.

Phase two was also in play if Rachel was successfully rescued. Jeremy accepted that as long as Shorey was alive there was no possibility of a safe life for him and his wife.

They drove in silence but the air inside the vehicle vibrated with nervous energy. While Tiberius remained quietly confident, Jeremy's own positivity with their chosen course of action had diminished significantly. He was starting to believe Tiberius' assessment that he had been in shock during the planning.

He also believed that he had no other choice.

Jeremy glanced at the rear view mirror, seeing Tiberius, but also noticing headlights behind him.

"Hey Ti, maybe I'm just nervous and paranoid, but I think there has been one car behind us since St. George."

Tiberius looked up from the weapons but didn't turn around.

"Okay. Take that right turn just after Bagatelle Great House. Let's see what happens."

Jeremy drove for another few minutes until he reached the turn, which connected onto a series of undulating, badly maintained roads surrounded by unkempt bushes. Even though a few homes dotted the landscape, the area was completely devoid of streetlights.

They drove for another fifteen seconds before Tiberius suggested stopping. Jeremy acquiesced, steering the SUV as far to the left as possible.

Tiberius handed Jeremy one of the Glocks, grabbed the Beretta and repositioned his body to look through the rear glass. Jeremy alternated his gaze between the rear view and side mirrors.

The sat quietly in this position for about two minutes.

Without streetlights, the moon bathed the area in a ghostly luminescence. They could hear the sound of traffic on the highway and periodically detected hints of the headlights from passing vehicles.

However, no vehicle had made the turn behind them.

"False alarm I guess," Jeremy whispered.

"Maybe, but you can never be too careful," Tiberius replied also under his breath. "Let's continue on this road. We can get back onto the highway through Mangrove."

They followed the twisting roads, passing a few tenantries and villages on the way, but primarily they were hedged-in by overflowing fields of tall sugar cane stalks approaching the end of their growing cycle.

As they turned West onto Mangrove Road they were assaulted by the scent emanating from the nearby landfill, which Barbadians had dubbed '*Mount Stinkeroo*' for obvious reasons.

"I don't know how people that live out here can stand this," Jeremy was saying as he cornered, when the headlights illuminated a pick-up truck parked lengthways across the road about one hundred feet away, blocking their path. Two men were on the far side of the vehicle, each brandishing a handgun.

"Don't stop Jeremy, ram them," Tiberius yelled from the backseat.

Jeremy pressed the accelerator and the Defender responded. They were moments from a collision when Jeremy's sense of self preservation kicked in.

He braked and pulled the steering wheel sharply to the left.

Tiberius, not wearing a seatbelt, swore as he was slammed against the right side of the vehicle. The SUV was filled with the sounds of the metal striking glass as the guns were tossed around.

The Defender cut a swath through the sugar cane field before coming to a stop fifty feet in. Jeremy hadn't pressed the clutch as he braked so the engine had sputtered and died.

Jeremy looked in the rear view mirror and saw that Tiberius was holding his head and looked a bit dazed. Jeremy turned and looked over his shoulder at him and noticed two figures outside approaching quickly from the road.

His heart was a jack hammer inside of his chest and adrenaline was causing him to tremble uncontrollably.

Tiberius saw Jeremy's expression and looked back. He swore again.

Jeremy tried to start the engine but in his panic continued to forget about the existence of the clutch, resulting in the vehicle bucking forward but nothing more. Tiberius swore again.

"Get this thing started JP," he snarled as he opened the door and leaped out of the SUV.

Jeremy looked back and saw Tiberius raise his weapon towards the approaching figures and pull the trigger. Nothing happened.

"Shit!" Tiberius muttered as he attempted to disengage the safety just as two explosions filled the air.

"No!" Jeremy yelled as he watched his friend spin backwards, dropping his gun and grabbing his chest. He made a few steps before a third gunshot caused Tiberius to arch his back and fall forward.

Jeremy looked on in horror for a moment before returning his attention to the ignition key. He finally remembered to press the clutch just as his door was pulled open and he was dragged from the SUV.

"Come here yuh rasshole," his assailant snarled as he threw Jeremy on the ground. He was now lying next to Tiberius whose face was buried in the freshly crushed sugar cane.

Jeremy looked up to see the silhouettes of two men looming over him.

"De man wanna talk to you," one of them said.

Jeremy struck out with his foot, catching the speaker on his shin. The man made a satisfying yelp as he dropped to one knee.

Jeremy turned and tried to drag himself up when he got a glimpse of a boot quickly approaching his head. His vision immediately exploded into millions of stars and then a second time as his head ricochetted off of the vehicle fender.

As he lay there, his head drowning in waves of almost indescribable agony, Jeremy was hyperaware of some of the odours around him. The sickly sweet smell of sugar cane was battling for dominance against the stench from the landfill. Both odours, however, were overwhelmed by the coppery aroma of blood.

He was thinking that he had smelt blood far too often in the last few days, when everything went black.

Chapter 13

West Indies vs Pakistan
Peshawar, Pakistan

Day 4 Report
*West Indies' batting crumbled once more as they went down
to their heaviest defeat against Pakistan.*

*The Caribbean team's batting lacked character, heart and
quality, while the bowling was adequate at best. They will
be embarrassed by their insipid overall performance.*

Thursday, November 20th, 1997

Jeremy and Tiberius arrived at The Outfield within minutes of each other, around five-thirty, immediately after work.

They sat at the bar and waited for Doc to come over. When the bartender saw them he automatically grabbed two Heinekens from the cooler and approached them, but Tiberius shook his head vigorously.

"No, no, no my good man. No simple ale for me today," he said, feigning a British accent.

Doc briefly stopped in his tracks but continued when Jeremy gave him the '*come here*' wave and said, "I'll take both."

Doc deposited the bottles in front of Jeremy and turned to Tiberius. "So you changing up on me today?"

"Before I answer, do you remember we made a bet when I was here on Monday?"

Doc looked puzzled. "What bet you talking 'bout?"

"A bet about cricket, Doc. About West Indies in Pakistan, Doc. Ringing any bells?"

The puzzled look on Doc's face slowly morphed into understanding which was quickly replaced by a scowl.

"Yes, you remember now," Tiberius said cheerfully. "Well, the West Indies lost badly, so I believe that means that my first drink is on you. You think I gonna waste a free drink on beer?"

Doc sighed audibly. "What are you having, sir?"

"I'll have Johnny Walker Black and ginger ale. In fact, that will be my new first drink whenever you're on duty."

Doc shrugged and turned to prepare the drink while Tiberius erupted into loud peals of laughter. Jeremy shook his head and took a swig of one of his beers.

Tiberius swivelled his stool so he was facing Jeremy. "I forgot to tell you, I invited Fiona to join us. You'll finally get to meet her."

"Great," Jeremy replied. "I finally get to see that Snuffleupagus is real."

Tiberius sucked his teeth and Jeremy laughed.

"Actually I told Rachel that I would be here, so she may pass by as well," Jeremy said.

"Cool. We'll be on a double date with two freaky girls. I smell an orgy."

It was Jeremy's turn to suck his teeth.

Tiberius looked around the bar. "I don't see Fat-Suey anywhere, though. Doesn't look like she's on duty."

"Just as well. I think she and Rachel had some words last night."

"Huh," Tiberius said, just as Doc returned with the whisky mix and placed it in front of him. Tiberius immediately lifted the glass, tipped it dramatically towards the bartender and then sipped loudly. Doc rolled his eyes and walked away.

"How long do you plan on doing this to Doc?" Jeremy asked.

"Oh, I don't know," Tiberius answered with a shrug. "I guess until he drops dead of old age right here at the bar, where I'll still be drinking, cause as you know, I'm gonna live forever."

A few minutes later, Jeremy watched in the mirror behind the bar as an attractive young lady walked in and stood on the landing near the entrance. She was white, but her immediate comfort and apparent familiarity with the bar suggested she wasn't a tourist like Jeremy first assumed. Plus she was dressed in business attire.

She flipped her shoulder length red hair as she looked around and then headed towards where they were seated.

"Is that Snuffleupagus by any chance?" Jeremy asked.

Tiberius glanced at the mirror before swivelling his stool and standing.

"Hey Fiona," he said when she reached him and they exchanged kisses on the cheek. "This is my buddy Jeremy. Jeremy, Fiona." Jeremy rose and shook her hand.

Tiberius guided Fiona to sit where he had been moments before and he sat one down.

Before Jeremy had a chance to sit, he saw Rachel walking from the entrance towards him. Her short, grey skirt made him smile inwardly. She was smiling outwardly as she reached him.

"Hello Jeremy-Phillips-from-last-night-at-the-Outfield," she said and kissed him on the lips without warning, and then whispered, "I owed you that from last night."

Jeremy was grinning sheepishly as he turned and introduced Rachel to Fiona.

They ordered drinks for the ladies before shifting locations to a table where they were soon in the middle of entertaining banter. Fiona, who turned out to be a twenty-one year old legal assistant originally from Ireland, was a surprisingly witty story teller and had everyone in stitches.

They were contemplating whether they should order food and another round of drinks when a waitress seemed to almost materialise next to the table, causing Rachel to gasp audibly.

"Susan."

The others looked up to see Susan Farrell, one hand with a notepad and the other on her hip, scowling at Rachel.

"I thought you weren't on duty tonight," Rachel continued.

"That would a suit you good, nuh?" Susan replied, a little louder than required.

Rachel stood and walked towards her. "Let's chat outside," she said and placed her arm on her friend's shoulder. Susan shook it off.

"Uh uh, we don't got nothin' to chat 'bout. You stay here with yuh friends." Her volume was rising, and her language became more distinctly Bajan as her anger escalated. Both patrons and staff were now looking in her direction.

"Susan, calm down," Rachel said in a gentle but firm tone. "This isn't necessary."

Susan looked from Rachel to the three others at the table, her gaze lingering for a moment on Tiberius and then on Fiona. Then she returned her attention to Rachel.

"All o' wunna could kiss my fat ass," she screamed as she threw the notepad on the ground and stormed out of the bar.

Rachel started as if she wanted to follow her, but then returned to the table.

"Well, that was exciting," Fiona said.

"Yeah," Rachel responded sheepishly. "A bit too much excitement for me, though. I think I'm calling it an evening."

She exchanged goodbyes with the table and Jeremy offered to walk her outside.

In the carpark Rachel suddenly hugged Jeremy, burying her face in his shoulder. Jeremy hesitated briefly before hugging her back. They stayed like that for a while, saying nothing.

Eventually Rachel lifted her head and looked at Jeremy, tears filling her eyes. "I'm so sorry about that."

"Don't worry about it," Jeremy said under his breath.

"I feel so embarrassed."

"It wasn't your fault."

"It was, kind of. I didn't deal with this properly at all. I should have resolved everything last night."

She put her head on Jeremy's shoulder again. "Do you feel like company?" she asked quietly.

Jeremy's heart leapt. "Sure."

"Should I follow you?" Rachel asked.

"Yes," Jeremy said, not trusting his voice to say anything else.

Ninety minutes later, they were sitting in Jeremy's living room drinking coffee, freshly brewed in his stainless steel french press.

Rachel was curled up in the single seater while Jeremy sat on the near side of the adjacent sofa.

Rachel spoke at length about the Susan situation, apologising intermittently for the scene at The Outfield. She thought that Susan's recent erratic and jealous behaviour certainly spelled the end of their fling and probably their friendship.

"In the end it's all my fault. I should never have started anything with her. She always gets too clingy, too quickly."

"I saw a bit of that myself, actually," Jeremy revealed.

"Oh?" Rachel raised an eyebrow.

"Yeah. On Tuesday at the bar. She seemed to take an immediate liking for Tiberius after he paid her a few compliments."

Rachel was nodding. "She's like that. And you know what? After seeing us altogether this evening, she'll feel betrayed," she added with a sigh.

"You need to stop blaming yourself."

"I'm just not used to this type of drama. What about you? Any psycho exes in your past?"

Jeremy pondered. "Well, I was stalked by a hot girl once?"

"Oh really? When was that?"

"When I was at UWI," Jeremy said, referring to the University of the West Indies.

"Come on," she said with a laugh. "University pussy doesn't count, everyone's crazy at university."

Jeremy smiled. "Tiberius said almost exactly the same thing yesterday at the shooting range."

"Shooting?" Rachel exclaimed. "I have to admit that surprises me. You don't seem like the gun toting type."

"I'm not really, but Tiberius is into guns these days so as his best buddy, I guess that makes me into guns."

Rachel smiled. "Do you own a gun?"

Jeremy shook his head. "I wouldn't be comfortable with one in the house."

"I see." Rachel sipped from her mug, her eyes slightly hooded as she looked at him.

"So if you're not armed, and I am a damsel in distress, how would you rescue me?"

Jeremy looked back at her, blinking slowly.

"I never said I wasn't armed," he said suggestively.

"You're right. You didn't. So you're saying you *can* rescue a fair maiden in distress," she said, batting her eyelids.

"I don't know," Jeremy said lowering his tone. "Maybe I should practise rescuing you right now."

Rachel put down her mug and got up to join Jeremy on the sofa, her short skirt riding up to expose well toned thighs.

"I am willing…"

She kissed Jeremy on the lips softly.

"…and able…"

She nibbled on his neck.

"…to help you practice."

Jeremy lifted her face towards his and kissed her, gently at first and then with increasing intensity.

She returned his passion, her tongue invading his mouth like a slow moving wave.

Jeremy caressed her shoulder and then let one hand trail lightly down her fully clothed body. He lingered on her breast before continuing down, followed the curve of her backside and then squeezed her exposed upper thigh.

Rachel moaned into his mouth and adjusted her position so that her body was pressed closer against his. She could feel his stiffening member throbbing against her thigh through his slacks. She reached down and cupped it firmly. They both moaned.

Jeremy pulled his mouth away from hers and pushed himself back into a seated position. "Come with me," he panted and stood up holding out his hand.

"I intend to," she said hoarsely and placed her hand inside of his, allowing herself to be led.

They quickly reached the darkened bedroom and Jeremy guided her into a lying position on the bed, kissing her deeply on the way down.

He started undressing her slowly, nibbling and kissing each area of flesh from which an article of clothing had been removed, provoking a series of moans and shudders from Rachel.

He removed her french cut underwear and with her left leg still in the air, gently sucked her toes, feeling her stiffen initially and then relax.

Slowly he ran his tongue across her instep and ankle, past her calf, the back of her knee and continued down her thigh, never losing contact with her skin.

She started to grind her pelvis forward in anticipation, her breathing becoming deeper and laboured.

When his tongue reached her wet pubic area she immediately grabbed the back of his head as involuntary tremors started to overwhelm her.

Less than a minute later the grip on his head tightened as her entire body stiffened. She arched her back while her mouth opened wide in a soundless scream.

She lay there breathing heavily while Jeremy stood up and hurriedly removed his clothes.

He grabbed a tie from the wardrobe doorknob, knowing it was the blue and grey one he wore when he first met Rachel three nights before.

He lowered himself next to her. "Hold out your hands," he whispered.

The faint moonlight streaming through the window was just enough to illuminate her face which betrayed a delicate mixture of confusion and desire.

She timidly lifted her hands towards Jeremy who bound them lightly with the tie.

"*Now* you're a damsel in distress," Jeremy whispered. "And I'm going to rescue you."

Jeremy kissed her as he climbed on top and started his rescue mission.

He rescued her three times in the next two hours.

Chapter 14

West Indies vs Australia
St. John's, Antigua

Day 5 Report
Omari Banks and Vasbert Drakes propelled West Indies to a nerve-wracking three-wicket victory on the final morning in Antigua.

Banks showed maturity beyond his 20 years, as he and Drakes knocked off the 47 runs that remained of the highest fourth-innings chase in Test history.

History had been made today in the most thrilling way possible.

Tuesday, May 13th, 2003

Jeremy saw nothing. Heard nothing. The smell of blood filled his nostrils. Its flavour flooded his mouth.

His head throbbed with a dull ache. He tried to move his right hand towards the pain but it refused to cooperate.

He attempted to open his eyes and was immediately rewarded with shards of agony piercing his brain while waves of nausea coursed through his body. A groan escaped his lips.

Then he did hear something. Rustling, like fabric on fabric. Then another sound.

"Jeremy."

It was Rachel's voice.

Soft hands touched his face.

"Jeremy."

He tried to open his eyes again, slowly this time, riding the waves of nausea and pain.

At first his vision was obscured by black and white flashes, but they dissipated gradually, partially revealing his wife's face.

"Rachel," he said huskily, his voice barely recognisable.

Tears flowed from her eyes. "Oh my God, you're awake. I didn't know…" She sobbed. "Sometimes I couldn't tell if you were breathing."

"Are you okay, Rachel?" It came out as a croak.

Rachel looked down at him for a few moments. "Yes," she answered unconvincingly.

"Your toe?" Jeremy asked, suddenly remembering the delivery from Shorey.

Rachel closed her eyes. "I'll be fine."

Jeremy tried to move his head, an action that was met with new pulses of pain and nausea.

"Where are we?" he asked.

"Barry's house."

Jeremy was finally able to raise his hand to his aching head and winced when his fingers made contact.

He tried to get up and Rachel cradled his head as he slowly pushed himself into a sitting position, fighting the worst headache ever all the way up.

His vision was still spotty and his head was spinning, but he could now see that he was sitting on a carpeted floor in a small, dimly lit, windowless room. The only piece of furniture was a bar stool in the centre. There was one door with a glass portal, the other side of which was complete darkness.

At first Jeremy thought that the carpet extended up the walls, before he recognised what he was looking at.

"Are we in a recording studio?"

Rachel nodded. "And it's underground."

His vision improving, Jeremy turned to look at his wife.

Her left eye was blackened and her lip swollen. There was an angry bruise on her left cheek, and another one on her throat that looked like a hand print.

She was still wearing the green T-shirt she wore to the Shell station on Sunday, but it was now badly torn. The yoga pants she had been wearing were gone, revealing a series of welts down both legs. Her left foot was wrapped in a green blood-stained bandage, which Jeremy quickly realised was made from strips of the T-shirt she was wearing.

Tears filled Jeremy's eyes. Rachel saw this and hugged him, crying outright.

Jeremy looked over her shoulder at his wrist and realised he was no longer wearing a watch. "How long have I been here?"

Rachel continued hugging him. "It's difficult to keep track of time down here, but it must be more than eight hours. Maybe more than ten."

"Ten hours," Jeremy repeated. "How did I even…"

Jeremy stopped talking when the details of the previous night started to drift into his memory.

"Tiberius," was all he said.

"What?"

"They killed Tiberius."

Rachel looked at him with an expression of resignation on her face.

"Jeremy, I think they're going to kill us too."

They were quiet for a while and at Jeremy's prompting, Rachel started to describe her experience since Sunday.

When she returned from the Shell station and stepped out of the SUV, she saw a wallet on the ground. As she bent down to retrieve it, she was grabbed from behind, a hand placed over her mouth, and hustled into a car. She was gagged and blindfolded until they reached their location.

"When the car stopped they told me that I was to walk with them into the house without causing a scene, otherwise they would kill me and then you. They removed the blindfold and gag and they took me inside through a side door. I was so scared."

She starting crying and Jeremy squeezed her hand.

"But I've been here before," she whispered through her sobs. "Not inside, but I delivered Barry's Range Rover here two years ago so I know it's his house."

"What happened when you got inside?"

Rachel took a deep breath. "They brought me to this room and started questioning me about Susan. They think we killed her and stole stuff, and even though I told them over and over that we didn't, they just kept hurting me and…"

She looked down at her left foot and started to cry again. New tears formed in Jeremy's eyes.

"I don't know why they think we had anything to do with this," she said through the tears.

"Because Susan told Shorey that she thought we wanted to hurt and rob her."

Rachel looked incredulous. "She did what?"

Jeremy then described his meeting with Shorey before updating her on everything that happened since then.

When he started to explain the plan Tiberius and he had devised, a feeling of extreme guilt washed over him. He realised now that they had been completely wrong about where Rachel was being held and the ill-conceived rescue mission had failed before it even began. His oldest and closest friend was killed as a result of him treating a serious and dangerous situation as if it was a game.

He eventually stopped speaking, trying to stave off the shame and sorrow that started to envelop him.

He looked at Rachel who's attention seemed to be elsewhere, with a curious expression on her face.   She then spoke under her breath.

"That bitch, Susan. She set us up. How could she do this to me?"

Jeremy looked at his wife and shrugged.

A muffled, rubbing sound startled them.

They turned to see the door swing outwards, revealing a young, dark skinned man whose face Jeremy recognised from the Haynesville Community Centre newspaper article.   Either Patrick Blackman or Jabari Forde from Shorey's inner circle.

He stepped into the room followed by Shorey, who walked past him and sat on the barstool.

"Good morning JP," he said cheerfully.   "I'm glad you've decided to join us. I wondered whether you would ever regain consciousness."

Jeremy didn't respond.

"So you went adventuring yesterday. Didn't turn out so well for you did it. At least you fared better than your friend."

Jeremy glared at Shorey without reacting, his face starting to feel hot from his attempt to keep his emotions in check.

Shorey leaned forward and when he spoke again, there was nothing but menace in his voice.

"This is what is going to happen today. One of you *will* tell me where my fuckin' money is, right, or body parts getting chop off 'till I know. You feeling me?"

They stared at him in horror.

"We don't know anything about any money," Rachel pleaded.

Shorey acted as if she hadn't spoken. He stood and looked at his watch.

"I am a man of my word," he said, his threatening tones completely vanished. "It's only nine fifty-five. You still have until two-thirty this afternoon to tell me what I need to know."

He then looked at his henchman who smiled sheepishly and shrugged.

"Furthermore, my friends tell me they want to watch cricket this morning on my big screen TV."

He returned his gaze to Jeremy. "I don't know if you had time for cricket updates yesterday when you were out playing hero, but the West Indies might actually win this thing. You're missing out on history, man."

Shorey walked away, but turned when he reached the door. "I wonder if your friend will be watching the game from the afterlife this morning." He chuckled and exited, followed by his henchman who pulled the door closed.

In the short time since Jeremy had regained consciousness he had experienced a range of emotions. Now anger come to the fore.

With Rachel's help he managed to lift himself into a standing position, resisting the urge to throw up. Using the wall as support he walked to the door and tried the handle, not expecting it turn. It didn't.

He scanned around the edges of the door and noted that it was built like a submarine's with a metallic lip surrounding the frame. This enhanced the security and soundproof qualities of the room.

He peered through the door portal into the adjacent room which was in darkness. The dim lighting of his current prison was enough to make it difficult to see through the glass but after squinting for a while he discerned what looked like the outlines of a refrigerator and stove.

"There's a kitchen out there," Jeremy said without turning.

"Yeah," came his wife's quiet despondent voice.

Jeremy looked around and found Rachel slumped on the barstool, eyes focussed on the floor. He followed her gaze and for the first time noticed the darker, irregularly shaped spot on the carpet, triggering images of his wife's toe being removed violently.

He pushed it out of his mind and walked around inspecting the walls, looking closer at the soundproofing foam that covered everything. He tried to tear a section away from the wall without success, so he slapped his hand against it, resulting only in a muffled thud.

Jeremy stared at the foam and remembered that he and Tiberius had discounted Shorey's home as a possible target because it was in a residential area and not ideal for a prison. He spiralled into guilt and grief once more.

He turned and leaned against the wall and then allowed himself to slide down until he settled on the carpet. He looked around and understood that this underground, soundproof room was the perfect prison. Sound could not escape, and neither could they it seemed.

Rachel joined him, putting her head on his shoulder.

They were seated like that for about thirty minutes when the door opened and Adrian stepped into the room, his expression an inscrutable scowl as usual.

He glared at the couple for a few moments before putting his hand in his pants pocket and fishing out something which he tossed towards them.

It landed on the carpet with a dull thud and at first Jeremy couldn't process what he was looking at.

"My keys," Rachel gasped finally.

Jeremy slowly recognised the metallic key fob bearing the Land Rover logo. Two keys were attached by a ring - one for a car and the other for a house.

They looked up at Adrian, making no attempt to move towards the keys.

Adrian continued to scowl in their direction. He then spoke with a throaty whisper.

"I gine leff this door unlock.   Go tru de kitchen and outside. Everybody upstairs watching cricket so yuh gine be good. Yuh gine see de car park down the gap when yuh get out.".

The couple continued to stare at Adrian in distrust and disbelief.

Adrian's expression softened slightly. He looked at Jeremy and spoke quietly.

"Look skipper, you did always good to we. You didn't have to fix my mother house or come to she funeral."

Jeremy looked closer at Adrian, comprehension creeping into his brain.

"And you used to talk to she, not like dem unmannerly people you does work fuh."

Jeremy's mouth fell open. "Adrian. Adrian Barrett," he whispered incredulously, remembering the young man with the red scarf on his head, riding a bicycle that was too small for an adult past his office.

Adrian was still speaking.

"I leffing 'bout here right now. If I did you, I would leff too."

With that, Adrian stepped back outside and pushed the door shut.

Jeremy and Rachel looked at each other and then the keys. After a few seconds Jeremy grabbed them and allowed Rachel to assist him to his feet.

They walked to the door hesitantly, Jeremy noticing Rachel limping and wincing with each step.

He tried the handle, which turned without a sound. Jeremy pushed the door open.

It took a moment for Jeremy's eyes to adapt fully to the darkness. He could now see a table with four chairs in the middle of the room, a microwave oven and coffee maker on a counter which terminated into the stove and refrigerator he had seen earlier.

There were two sets of stairs leading out of the room - one directly ahead of where they stood and the other to the far left.

Suddenly Jeremy and Rachel were startled by a chorus of yells.

After a heart stopping few seconds they realised that the sound came from a distance beyond the steps in front of them. Jeremy reckoned it was the guys watching cricket upstairs.

Rachel was pushing him toward the left side staircase.

They slowly made their way in that direction, Rachel still walking with difficulty, Jeremy still feeling the effects of his head trauma.

They supported each other up the stairs, following delicate beams of light streaming through the narrow spacing around the door above them.

At the top, Jeremy gently held the door knob and twisted. It turned easily so Jeremy pushed and then pulled but the door did not budge.

"Wait," Rachel whispered as reached past him and turned the locking mechanism under the knob. Then Jeremy pushed again and the door opened, flooding the stairway with sunlight.

Squinting his eyes and fighting renewed agony in his head, along with the panic that threatened to propel his heart out of his chest, Jeremy stepped outside.

He discovered that he was at the side of the house, which appeared to be on a cul-de-sac.

He peered around the liquified petroleum gas cylinders just outside the door and scanned the area quickly, seeing no-one. Through an upstairs window he detected the faint sound of the guys watching the game.

He looked towards the entrance of the property and in the distance saw the Defender parked at the side of the road, about two hundred feet away.

He beckoned for his wife to join him and they slowly started following a path to the entrance. After a few steps he stopped suddenly.

"What?" Rachel whispered.

Jeremy didn't answer but looked at his wife, not seeing for a moment.

His mind was racing.

He realised that the second phase of the plan still needed to be completed. He still needed to kill Barrington Shorey. Otherwise they would never be safe again.

Jeremy looked down at the key fob he was holding and quickly made a decision.

He hastily removed the keys from the metallic fob, breaking his thumb nail in the process. He gave the keys to Rachel.

"Do you think you can make it to the car by yourself?

Rachel looked towards the Defender and then back to Jeremy.

"Yes but why?"

"Go ahead. I'm coming in a sec."

"Where are you going?" Rachel whispered frantically.

"I have to fix this. Go. I'll be there shortly."

With that he turned and headed back to the basement. When he reached the entrance he look back at Rachel who hadn't moved.

"Go!" he mouthed silently.

She hesitated, but then turned and started limping towards the SUV, looking conspicuous in her torn green shirt and by the absence of pants or shoes.

Jeremy left the door open and walked carefully downstairs, the sunlight behind him illuminating the room.

He headed straight for the stove and inspected it briefly to confirm that it was gas powered, an assumption he had already made when he saw the gas cylinders outside.

He then proceeded to turn on all four top burners. He opened the oven and noted the pilot light at the bottom. He crouched down and blew it out, then turned on the oven and left it open.

A noxious odour was already filling the room, intensifying his nausea.

Jeremy stepped to the microwave, opened it and put the metallic key fob inside. After a brief pause he carefully pulled open a drawer under the counter and grabbed a handful of silver utensils. He placed them in the microwave as well.

He closed the door, set the timer for fifteen minutes and pressed start.

The appliance hummed into life, causing Jeremy to freeze in place, momentarily thinking that the sound would alert his former captors upstairs.

He watched through the glass for a few moments as the Land Rover logo slowly rotated among the small pile of knives and forks, before he shook himself out of his inertia and walked quickly to the stairs.

He reached the top and closed the door quietly behind him.

Looking down the street he could see the Defender in the distance with Rachel leaning on the driver's side door, looking back at him with a panicked look on her face.

Jeremy started jogging towards her and covered about fifty feet when he was finally overcome by the nausea that had threatened since he regained consciousness.

He fell to his knees and vomited violently, bringing up nothing but liquid and bile.

He tried to get up but found that the convulsions wracking his body made it impossible.

"Jeremy!" he heard his wife screaming. He looked up and realised she was limping towards him.

"No," he struggled to say, when he heard a shout behind him.

"What de rasshole?"

He looked back and briefly saw the man that Tiberius described as a '*Syrian looking dude*' in an upstairs window, disappearing almost immediately.

"Ishmael Mansour," Jeremy muttered just as the world became a ball of fire behind him.

Then he was rolling, tumbling down the street.

There was no sound. It was like he was in the cell again. But there was heat and light. The world was heat and light.

He came to rest next to his wife who was sitting in the street looking past him with her eyes and mouth wide open.

She then looked down at Jeremy, her lips moving to form words he couldn't hear.

He looked up at her, his brain feeling like it was painfully trying to escape the confines of his skull.

"We won," was all he managed as his world dissolved into blackness for the second time in twelve hours.

It was still dark and quiet.

But not completely silent like before.

Jeremy could hear a soft electric hum. Was it a refrigerator? No. It was above him. Florescent lights?

The distant sound of a car horn drifted in. He found the presence of traffic relaxing somehow.

Were those crickets? So it's probably nighttime then.

He started counting the cricket chirps to work out the temperature but became distracted by a gentle snoring nearby.

He opened his eyes slowly, expecting another assault of agony. He was surprised by the lack of pain. In fact, there was a lack of sensation of any kind.

The florescent lamps came into focus above him. Then the sterile, sparsely decorated room.

He glanced down to find himself shirtless but covered in scratches and strips of white bandages. A needle was stuck into his left arm and held in place by tape. His eyes followed the tube to the plastic bag of liquid hanging next to him.

Jeremy thought that whatever was in that bag must be of exceptional quality because he was feeling nothing.

Another snore.

He looked to his right and saw Rachel lying in a bed six feet away.

She was covered by a blanket and also attached to an intravenous drip. Her left leg was elevated and covered with fresh bandages.

She looked at peace.

"You're up."

Jeremy turned his head slowly to the left towards the voice and saw Detective Harold Mason walking into the room.

"Detective," he tried to say but it came out as a harsh whisper.

"Don't try to talk Mr. Phillips. I just came by to check on you."

Mason walked over to the right side of the bed, looked at Rachel for a moment before turning his attention to Jeremy.

"I understand your wife has a bit of a foot injury, but she's going to be fine. You both are."

Jeremy nodded.

"I also wanted to let you know that the home of Barrington Shorey was completely destroyed this morning. The first responders are still combing the wreckage but so far four bodies have been found. It appears that Shorey and most of his cohorts have perished."

Mason looked at Jeremy, who didn't react.

"There was damage to neighbouring homes but not substantially so. And there were no other injuries, other than the two of you."

Mason paused and looked over at Rachel again. "You and your wife were very lucky."

"Tiberius?" Jeremy asked hoarsely.

Mason hesitated, looking uncomfortable as he considered his answer. He looked at the floor and cleared his throat before responding.

"I'm afraid Mr. James was not as fortunate. I am so sorry."

Jeremy nodded and closed his eyes.

"I'll let you get some rest Mr. Phillips. When you've suitably recovered, you can make an official statement. Sleep well."

As Mason walked away Jeremy opened his eyes.

"Detective."

Mason stopped at the door and turned.

"What happened… cricket?" Jeremy asked, barely above a whisper.

Mason's face was expressionless for a few moments before dissolving into a grim half-smile.

"West Indies made history."

The small fishing vessel made its way though the dark velvet waters of the Caribbean Sea.

Hints of moonlight peeking through the gathering clouds sparsely illuminated the ocean, giving everything an otherworldly quality.

Adrian Barrett steered the boat with the deft hand of someone with years of experience making drug runs between the islands. He looked at the clouds ahead.

"A storm coming, yeah."

Susan Farrell was lying on the deck, her head propped on a large dark coloured duffel bag which currently held over two million dollars in US currency.

"Ok," she said weakly, making no attempt to move.

Adrian turned to look at her. "You sure you good?"

Susan looked down at her left hand, which was bandaged from wrist to bicep. They had decided to get all the blood they needed for their deception in one go, so that there would have been no evidence of it on her body before she disappeared. If Barry had found needle marks on her at any time, he would have assumed she was using his product and that would not have ended well for her.

However, taking so much blood at one time had been a mistake. Her body had almost shut down. It meant they couldn't leave for St. Lucia on Friday night as planned, but instead she had been recovering in the St. Silas Heights show home, where Adrian lived, for four days.

"I'll be fine," she said quietly.

Through her discomfort she smiled at the realisation that she had successfully executed a plan that was two years in the making.

She got her money, she got her man and she fixed that bitch Rachel.

"Rachel should be dead by now, right?" she asked.

Adrian didn't answer immediately.

He didn't know anything that happened after he left Shorey's house that morning, and he also hadn't told Susan that he had given Jeremy and Rachel the means to escape.

"I guess so," he answered softly.

Susan chuckled weakly.

"That bitch knew for two whole years that I did planning on robbing Barry, but she didn't know I would set she to rass up."

She laughed again, weaker this time.

"Feel she could just throw me 'way and I do nothing," she muttered quietly and turned on her side, her eyes closed.

Adrian said nothing. He looked at the clouds forming ahead.

They were definitely heading towards a storm.

Epilogue

Rachel and Susan had finished dinner and were having drinks at the Cloverleaf Lounge.

They had confirmed that they would be getting together with Jeremy the following night for a special erotic experience. They giggled like schoolgirls at the exciting prospect of a threesome.

The restaurant was quieter than usual so they were enjoying the mellow reggae music while they drank.

"I can't believe how good you look, Susan Farrell. All toned and shit. I'm so jealous."

Susan grinned. "Don't be silly. I wish I could look as gorgeous as you."

They stared at each other for a few seconds before Rachel broke eye contact and took a sip of her drink.

"So Susan, where are you working these days?"

"I'm not really working at the moment, but I occasional help out a friend and it pays."

"Help out a friend, huh. Whore."

They both laughed.

"Come on Susan, you're not a teenager anymore. What's the long term plan?"

Susan's expression became serious.

"I actually do have a plan, but I know you won't approve."

"You know me better than that. I never judge."

Susan sipped her drink and stared at Rachel.

"Okay, it's like this. My friend has a business where large quantities of money end up lying around. My plan is to wait for the right moment, take the money, go back home to St. Lucia and live like a queen."

Rachel stared at her with a shocked look on her face.

"Are you crazy? What sort of plan is that?"

"It's a great plan if I play it right. And I can cut you in if you want. It's just like jobs we used to pull back in the day. Just much bigger."

Rachel settled back in her seat.

"Thanks Susan, but you know I've left that life behind." She smiled broadly.

"Jeremy has made an honest woman out of me in more ways than one."

Susan looked away for a moment before returning her attention to Rachel, smiling.

"Suit yourself, sweetie. More for me."

"When do you plan on pulling this job, anyway?"

Susan shrugged. "I don't know. I have to plan it properly and play it really safe. May be a while."

"Ok. Just be careful."

Rachel then picked up the menu. "I just remembered, I have to order some dessert for JP."

"The cheesecake is good here," Susan said flatly.

They sat in silence for a while after that, enjoying the ambiance and the music. The lovers rock classic, *Silly Games* by Janet Kay, was playing.

Susan listened to the lyrics and smiled.

"This is one of my favourite songs," she said and started to sing along.

A Few Words From The Author

Games started out as a short story in 1999. That first chapter with Jeremy breaking into his own house was the entire thing - just me trying my hand at writing something set in Barbados that wasn't essentially Barbadian in content.

I forgot about the story until around 2010 when I rediscovered the document and wondered what else would happen in the world of Jeremy and Rachel. I also thought it would be interesting to write about middle class Barbadians, who I thought were underrepresented in Bajan literature.

After thinking about it for months I finally devised a storyline that excited me. I wrote most of the second chapter before life got in the way of the project, prompting a writing sabbatical. However the story was never far from my thoughts.

Sometime in 2014, I had the revelation of tying the narrative to West Indies cricket and using that to differentiate between different time periods. From there, the story unfolded in a different way from how I originally envisioned but I was excited again.

I wrote steadily, if not quickly for the next few years, until a productive spurt in mid-2018 allowed me to finally finish the thing.

I had some help along the way.

All of my friends who I forced to read unfinished manuscripts over the years and who also convinced me that it was worth finishing - I thank all of you.

I have to thank Branford for helping me with the legal questions that formed the basis of some of Detective Mason's dialogue and motivation.

Nikita's suggestions really helped me to work out several elements of the story's final act and I am grateful.

Theo, you showed me that this could be done and inspired me to push through to the end.

And finally, Danielle you were always there to encourage and sometimes push me. I wouldn't have done this without your continuous positive reinforcement and I dedicate this novel to you.

Kayio Beckles
July 22nd, 2018

Printed in Great Britain
by Amazon

25037421R00155